A MEMORABLE LITTLE MEMORIAL DAY

A Holidays at Rawhide Ranch Story

HONEY MEYER

©All rights reserved.

This is a work of fiction. Names, characters, businesses, places, events, and incidents are either the products of the author's imagination or used in a fictitious manner. Any resemblance to actual persons, living or dead, or actual events is purely coincidental.

No part of the book may be reproduced or transmitted in any form or by any means, electronic or mechanical, including photocopying, recording, or by any information storage and retrieval system, without permission in writing from the publisher.

2022 © Published by Honey Meyer

Holidays at Rawhide Ranch

A Memorable Little Memorial Day

Edited by Manu Velasco of Tessera Editorial

Cover by AllyCat's Creations

This book is intended for adults only. Spanking and other sexual activities represented in this book are fantasies only, intended for adults. Nothing in this book should be interpreted as the author's advocating any non-consensual spanking/sexual activity or the spanking of minors.

For more Rawhide Ranch stories check out this link-
https://linktr.ee/Rawhide

CHAPTER 1

"Why do you hate me so much?" Maddie groaned, trying to cover her head with a pillow.

It was still dark, and it was unreasonable that her so-called friend Tamsyn was trying to pry her out of bed. Friends didn't drag friends out of nice warm beds before the butt crack of dawn on a Saturday. They just didn't.

"I don't hate you. I love you. Which is why we're going on a big trip before I move away."

Maddie didn't put up a fight when Tamsyn stripped the pillow out of her hands. Instead, Maddie looked into her bestie's hazel eyes with the saddest puppy dog pout she could muster.

"You moving away proves for real that you hate me," she asserted. "If you really loved me, you'd stay here forever. We could buy a house and get old together. The neighborhood kids would speculate that we were lesbian witches. It would be great."

"It would be great. But neither of us are lesbians." Tamsyn's wink did little to make her feel better.

"Potay-to, potah-to. We could be witchy enough to make up for the not-lesbians thing."

"Know what we couldn't be witchy enough for?"

Maddie sighed and rolled her eyes. "Conjuring money out of thin air?"

"Exactly. So, while I love you to bits, and I wish you'd reconsider moving with me..."

Maddie shook her head.

"Well, see, now who doesn't love who? I can't advance any higher in my company without working out of HQ, and I can't make more money without a promotion. Not really. So Clover City, here I come. You, though..."

Ugh, she hated the way Tamsyn was looking at her, the raised eyebrow and the pursed lips. Made her feel like she was being stubborn and irrational. Which she probably was, but she didn't like being reminded of it.

"Fine, fine. I'm getting up, are you happy now?"

"I'll be happier when you're showered and dressed and we're on the way to Montana."

At the reminder of where they were headed, Maddie flopped back onto her bed.

"Ah, no you don't! Time to get up. Don't make me get the hose, Madigan Rose Arsenault."

"Why couldn't we go someplace normal for our trip? Like New York? Or Vegas? Or the beach?"

Maddie knew she was being whiny, but she really was not looking forward to being away from Penshaw for so long. Or at all. Tamsyn had had to beg her *pretty please* for weeks to get her to agree to go anywhere; then it took another few to convince her to go to Montana—and to a ranch, of all places. What the heck.

Then her friend was flopping down next to her, on her stomach instead of her back.

"Would it have been easier to convince you to go somewhere else?"

It was very irritating to have a friend who made sense so often. Maddie scowled but had to concede. "No."

"Then, Rawhide Ranch in Montana, here we come. Maybe we'll even find you a nice cowboy to ride."

Maddie groaned and reached for the pillow again, but Tamsyn beat her to it.

"Come on, you. Let's get a move on. Let's make our last week together a memorable one."

Maddie could've argued that this would not be their last week together. She might've accepted that Tamsyn wouldn't be living in Penshaw anymore, but that didn't mean her bestie would never come to town ever again. Hey, she might even go visit her in Clover City. Probably not, but anything was possible.

But she'd given her roommate and BFF a hard enough time this morning, and she didn't want to actually ruin the trip Tamsyn had worked so hard to plan.

"Fine, fine, fine. But can I at least have some strawberry Pop-Tarts before we go to the airport?"

"With sprinkle frosting and everything," Tamsyn agreed.

Well, everything was still awful, but at least it would be chock-full of sugar. That would just have to do.

* * *

"Why do you hate me?" Reid muttered as he slung his duffel bag and play kit into the back seat of his friend Fitz's club cab pickup.

"Heard that. And I hate you because you're an asshole."

"Y'ever think I wouldn't be such an asshole if you

weren't dragging me halfway across the state to spend a week at a ranch when I grew up on a goddamn ranch? A ranch isn't fun; a ranch is hard labor. It's getting up early and breaking your back and still getting undercut by corporate assholes. A ranch is where you work your fingers to the bone and still die with nothing but your land to show for it. It's not someplace you go for a vacation."

A ranch was also where he'd disappointed his folks when he'd told them he was leaving. So while he understood the appeal to people who didn't know any better and didn't have bad memories attached to such places, they were about as far from his idea of paradise as he could get. Fitz knew that.

"No," Fitz said with a shrug.

Reid couldn't argue that. He'd been a grumpy asshole for months now. Fitz knew that too. Also knew why and would remind him of it in three, two, one...

"Not my fault you've fucked your way through the county and now you can't get laid."

There it was. Something else Reid couldn't argue about. While it wasn't *exactly* true, he had dated or at least slept with almost all the single women in Franklin County, so it was getting close. Unlike some people, he wasn't going to start messing around with the taken ladies, and there also weren't a whole lot of eligible women moving into the area. Not much of anyone, really, but especially not single women in his generous age range.

"So this is a pity-fuck trip?"

"Insofar as I pity the women who fuck you," Fitz shot back. Who was the asshole now?

He knew his friend was joking, but the comment still rankled. It's not like he was some Casanova intent on racking up notches on his bedpost or otherwise proving his masculinity with his dick. It's just... Well, he was kind of a fuckboy, and was that really any better?

His parents, his father especially, had always said he had the attention span of a gnat. Was it Reid's fault if that applied to women as well as to school? To the myriad jobs he'd held? His habit of picking up and moving at least every other year? Reid didn't think so. For better or worse, that was just how he was built.

"Hey, I don't hear any complaints," he told his friend as they settled into the cab of the truck for the long drive to Rawhide Ranch.

If anything, he prided himself on showing his partners a good time. They seemed to appreciate the body he'd earned through a lifetime of work on his parents' ranch and now with lifting and hauling at Mason's Motors, plus hiking and fishing and pretty much anything else that would get him outside. He'd also been told he had a laid-back cowboy charm that made women feel comfortable. Certainly seemed that way when they were blushing and giggling and flirting with him out at the bars or over the popped hoods of their cars.

And last but definitely not least, having had a lot of partners had given him a pretty big toolbox to figure out what was going to get any individual woman off. Some of them liked to be seduced with sweet, soft words murmured in their ears and deep sensual kisses that led to him licking his way down their bodies and worshiping their pretty pussies. Some of them liked to be manhandled—tossed over his shoulder, a few swats on their backsides, some hair pulling, and a firm hand around their throat while he fucked them senseless. Yeah, there were all kinds of women with all kinds of wants and needs, and he did his best to have them all calling out his name in ecstasy.

"Probably because you never stick around long enough to hear anything at all," Fitz observed.

Reid grunted and leaned forward to turn the radio up. Fitz had been a real good friend to him for a long time, but that didn't mean he had to take the man's flak, especially when Fitz was the one who'd wanted to visit a goddamn kink ranch for a vacation.

"I think the peanut gallery's had enough to say for the day. How about you just shut up and drive, you ginger bastard?"

CHAPTER 2

The gates they rolled up to were pretty serious. Arched wrought iron with *Rawhide Ranch* in the center, flanked by a guard shack where they confirmed their reservations with a security guard. Once they were cleared, they still had to crunch over a long gravel drive past a bunch of outbuildings before they reached a sprawling resort building.

"Whoa, swanky," Maddie breathed.

"I know, right? We're going to have such a good time," Tamsyn said, almost bouncing on the back seat of the car she'd arranged to bring them here from the airport.

Once they'd stopped in front of the big front doors, their driver took their suitcases out of the trunk and carried them up the few steps to the main porch. Maddie and Tamsyn followed, and the massive doors swung open to reveal a bouncy brunette.

"Welcome to Rawhide Ranch, ladies!"

Wow, she was really excited. And looked like a stereotypical cowgirl in a skirt that was denim on the top and had tiers of brightly colored cotton fabric that went down to her knees and, of course, wore embroidered leather cowboy boots.

"Come on in and set your things down. I'll have Moses bring your bags to your room. You must be Tamsyn and Maddie, right? I thought you'd be arriving around now. I'm Sadie, the hostess. I'm married to Master Derek—you'll meet him soon enough, I'm sure. We own this place, so if you need anything, you let me know."

Master? Had she heard that right? That was odd. Maybe that was some kind of ranch jargon she didn't know about.

"Let's get you checked in," Sadie continued, rounding a big desk and typing some things into a computer. "Oh, that's right, you two are staying in a suite but also participating in a bunch of our Littles' activities. You're going to love it. We have a ton of special stuff planned for this Singles Mingle Memorial Day Week. Oh good, you're already signed up for a trail ride with a Littles' group tomorrow. Were there any specially themed dungeon nights you wanted to go to? I really like the pirate one. I hope Daddy won't make me walk the plank."

Sadie giggled, sounding like maybe she wouldn't mind that so much after all, and continued to chatter about all the activities and other features of the Ranch, but Maddie barely heard her. The *Master* thing, she could've blown off, but along with the rest? Tamsyn had some explaining to do. Like, a lot.

"What the hell kind of place did you bring me to?" Maddie sputtered.

Tamsyn looked at Sadie apologetically. "Can I have a minute with my friend?"

"Of course," the warm hostess said. "Take all the time you need. I'll circle back to check on you, or you can just give a shout whenever you're ready."

After Sadie bounced off to be chipper in someone else's direction, Tamsyn grabbed Maddie's hands, towed her over to a corner where they could talk more privately, and waited until Maddie stopped scowling at the rug and looked at her.

"Okay, so Rawhide Ranch isn't your typical ranch. It has horses and things, but it's also a BDSM resort. One of the best in the world. And in addition to all the usual impact play and bondage and other kinky stuff, they have a focus on age play."

All the blood drained from Maddie's face, but she tried to play it cool. There was no reason to think Tamsyn knew she was a Little. It's not as though she'd ever told her.

Yes, they shared almost everything, including that they were both not exactly vanilla, but they hadn't done a deep dive into those conversations. Why would they? Maddie hadn't been with anyone since Josh, and Tamsyn didn't date much—between putting in a ton of hours for work and the two of them being so close, her BFF didn't have much time.

Sensing Maddie didn't have anything to say right now, Tamsyn pressed on.

"I brought you here because this is going to be really fun. We're going to have a great time, and we're going to remember this trip for the rest of our lives."

"For one reason or another," Maddie grumbled, feeling salty as all heck. She didn't like making choices, but she also didn't like to be caught unaware.

"And I did it now because, even though I'm betting you're really going to enjoy this place, I thought you might need some space from me afterward. You're pretty mad at me right now. I get it. But I didn't think you'd agree to come here if I told you the truth, and I really wanted this for you. I love you exactly how you are, and I understand you better than you might think. You're a Little."

Maddie blinked at her friend, feeling like she'd been stripped naked and splashed with a bucket of ice water. "How did you...?"

Tamsyn shrugged. "It seems like life is easier for you when I'm telling you what to do. You get so overwhelmed by adulting. Which, like, same," she said with a chummy smile, "but it feels like being alive is harder for you than it is for me. And, besides me bossing you around, what seems to make you feel better are things like coloring and watching kids' movies, drinking hot cocoa and cuddling your stuffies, building pillow forts...things like that."

That was all true. And when her friend laid it all out like that, it didn't seem so surprising that Tamsyn had cottoned on to the fact that she was maybe kind of Little. But there was a big difference between knowing that about someone and then throwing them into a playpen for a vacation. How was this even supposed to work? This was a really big deal, and she felt completely unprepared.

"Okay, so I get to be Little for a week, and then I have to go home and be a grown-up?"

Maddie wasn't sure how she felt about that. While she sometimes did Little things, she hadn't been full-on Little since Josh. And the idea of jumping into the deep end of the pool for a week only to have to slog out of it and be left high and dry seemed almost more painful than just continuing to mostly ignore the wants and desires that burned inside her.

"Well, that's kind of up to you." Tamsyn's hazel eyes narrowed, and she wrenched her mouth to the side. "They have the Littles' dorms here, even a college. It's possible you could stay for longer. If you wanted to."

Oh. She hadn't realized that was a thing she could do. But even if being Little for a longer period of time was technically possible, it would probably cost a small fortune with room and board and everything else—a small fortune she definitely didn't have.

"Hey," Tamsyn said, taking Maddie's hands. "I see those gears grinding in that head. If you think that's something you need or really want, we'll figure out how to make it work. Master Derek is super protective of Littles, and he'd never turn away a Little girl in need."

Maddie had often felt needy in her life, and it wasn't something people usually liked about her. It was such an odd feeling to find herself at a place that might make all her most secret fantasies come true. Also deeply mortifying, but she knew Tamsyn was trying to take care of her, and she loved her friend for that.

"I also thought..." Tamsyn blew a breath out through her nose. "I also thought you might meet someone here. A Daddy."

Okay, Maddie had been pretty patient and understanding about the whole "being packed off to an age play resort without knowing" thing. Exhibit A: she was still standing in the lobby instead of making a break for the airport on foot. But meeting a Daddy? Too far. Maddie yanked her hands away and folded her arms over her chest.

"No."

The look Tamsyn gave her then was so full of pity it made Maddie want to throw things. Pity didn't do her any good. Nothing did. Because the only thing that would ever be able to fill this hole inside her was impossible. So she was just going to have to learn how to walk this earth with a soul like Swiss cheese. She'd figure out how to do that. Someday. Maybe.

"Maddie," Tamsyn said softly. "Josh has been gone for five years. I know you still miss him. I know you still love him. But that doesn't mean you have to be alone."

"Actually, it kinda does."

Sure, she'd thought about finding someone else in the intervening years, but something always stopped her from acting on it. Some mix of guilt, feeling as though she was betraying the only guy she'd ever loved, and fear. And not a small amount of hopelessness. No one would ever compare to Josh. How could they?

Tamsyn shook her head. "I'm not going to make you do anything you don't want to do, and neither is anyone else here. But—"

Ugh, there was always a *but*, wasn't there?

"But even if you don't want to or think you can't find a forever someone, you could have some fun for a week. Flirt, play, maybe get laid?"

"Oh my goodness," Maddie muttered into her hands as she covered her flaming face. "Please stop talking."

"I'll stop talking if you promise to at least try to have some fun this week. And also, if someone happens to catch your eye…"

No one would. Sure, from time to time, she would see men she found attractive, but they were nice to look at and nothing more. None of them called to her heart the way Josh had, no one lit the same spark she'd felt the first time she'd laid eyes on him. She'd been lucky enough to have one soul mate, no way she would happen upon a second—and definitely not at a kinky ranch.

"Fine. I promise to try to have some fun. And if, by some miracle, there is someone who's interested in me and I have even the tiniest shred of reciprocal interest, I promise not to stab him in the eye with a fork."

Tamsyn glared at her and set her hands on her hips. Had the nerve to tap her toe because she could be a drama queen like that.

"Look, that's as good as you're going to get, you manipulative worst best friend ever. Take it or leave it."

"Take it," Tamsyn decreed, smiling, then bounced toward her to link their arms. "Now let's go tell Sadie the good news."

CHAPTER 3

"You know, for a guy who doesn't like ranches, you've sure spent a lot of time down at the stables."

Fitz's observation over his omelette was obnoxious. Just like the rest of Fitz. Instead of answering him right away, Reid took another huge bite of his breakfast burrito and chewed it deliberately.

It was true that after they'd checked in, gotten settled in their room, and taken a brief tour of the Ranch yesterday, he'd walked back down to the paddocks where the livestock was kept—including a yard of turkeys that all seemed to have names—and found himself drawn to the stables.

The smells and sounds of horses were familiar, and he'd enjoyed a few hours looking over the animals and chatting with the crew who ran the place. Not that he wanted to interrupt their working because he understood maintaining horses took a lot of time and labor, and he didn't want to be a clueless guest who kept people from their tasks, but no one had seemed to mind talking with him for a bit.

The facilities were far nicer than his parents' place—no wonder, since they had guests wandering through who'd paid a pretty penny to be here—but it wasn't all for show. The animals were well cared for, and the people he'd met seemed to genuinely care for both the horses and the guests.

He'd probably register for a trail ride later in the week, but yesterday afternoon and evening, he'd enjoyed just hanging around the stables. He'd especially liked shooting the shit with a stable hand named Travis and his Little redheaded wife, Wren, who also worked the stables, and had a good time talking shop with the stable master, a big man named Jagger, who kind of reminded him of his father.

Reid had felt so at ease there, in fact, that he planned to head back to the stables after he and Fitz had finished inhaling their breakfasts. The food here so far had been top-notch, and there was plenty of it.

"Just because I wasn't cut out for ranch life doesn't mean I don't like horses. They shoot their mouths off a whole lot less than people do, that's for sure," he said pointedly.

Fitz grinned and dragged some home fries through a ridiculously huge puddle of ketchup before shoving them in his mouth.

"I'm just saying that while you're at a highly regarded BDSM resort, you might want to, I don't know, partake in some of that. Haven't you seen anyone around that interested you?"

Reid slathered some more guacamole onto his burrito and took another bite. Sure, he'd seen several attractive women around, and of course, there were the gaggles of Little girls running around the place. Well, more like being herded by various Bigs. The point was, there were plenty of women to have some fun with. And while fun was his usual

MO, he didn't feel like falling into bed with another pretty face. What the hell was wrong with him?

Maybe he just needed a breather, to unwind a bit before he got serious about finding a partner or three or however many women he could play with and/or fuck over the course of the week. He loved his job at Mason's, and he was real glad the old man had taken a chance on him when he had a resume a mile long from never staying in one place for more than a few months, but they'd been busy, and he'd been pulling a bunch of overtime. Probably needed to air out some of the gas and oil fumes from his brain and settle in a bit before going on the hunt. *Yeah, that must be it.*

Whatever it was, he didn't feel like having an impromptu psychotherapy session with Doctor Fitz. Especially since Fitz was actually a small-animal vet. So, instead of answering, he shot back, "Haven't you?"

Fitz shrugged. "Lots of good-looking women around. I'm sure we'll have fun at the play parties. For more than that? Who knows."

* * *

"Are you ready for some horsies?"

Tamsyn's voice punctuated the cloud of sleep she'd been floating in, and Maddie groaned. Why did her friend sound so chipper this early in the day? It was uncivilized.

"No."

"That's too bad because horsies are ready for you!"

"I've never been on a horse," Maddie whined.

"And that's exactly why we're going to go ride some. So you can't say that anymore. Didn't you have a horse phase when you were kid? I thought everyone did."

Maddie shrugged and then stretched, yawning deeply. "I did, but that doesn't mean I got to ride one."

"Well, today is your lucky day."

Luck was definitely a word, but Maddie wasn't at all sure it applied here.

"Come on, you don't want to be late. I hear Littles get spankings if they misbehave."

"I haven't misbehaved!" Maddie protested.

"Not yet. But I bet being late for our Littles' horsey lesson would count as misbehavior. Do you really want to find out?"

Ugh. As much as Maddie didn't want to get out of the nice warm bed, she also didn't want to get in trouble. She hated that yucky, creepy-crawly feeling in her stomach of having done something bad. She also was not excited about the prospect of being spanked by a stranger.

It had been one thing for Josh to take her over his knee and lecture her while he rained blows down on her backside. She knew he loved her, and they'd made an agreement that he could discipline her. An agreement that had taken months to hammer out and that she knew could be modified at any time if it wasn't working for either or both of them.

Maddie had never loved the fact physical punishment made an impression on her brain that nothing else did, but it was just how things were. And Josh had worked really hard to make her feel okay about that.

There was no way some rando baring her butt and hitting her would have the same effect as Josh's loving correction.

"No."

"I didn't think so. Now let's get ready for some horsies!"

Tamsyn chattered at her while she got dressed and

while they walked to the stables where the class would be. However else Maddie might feel about being here, she had to admit it was a beautiful place. So much big sky, so much open space. It felt free in a way Penshaw didn't. Maybe because her hometown was smack in the middle of the rust belt, a relic of better days for manufacturing and mom-and-pop main streets. Way past its prime, Penshaw was admittedly run-down and gritty. Most people who had the means to leave had. But not her.

There was already a knot of Littles at one of the riding rings when she and Tamsyn arrived, and they were all talking and shouting and giggling. Maddie had never been outgoing or boisterous, and her shyness had turned into an affect some people might label *withdrawn*.

Her bestie knew better and tried to urge her toward the rowdy crowd.

"Come on, Maddie. You could at least tell someone you like their outfit."

She definitely did. Everyone looked so cute, and she felt out of place in her clothes that were just sort of...clothes. A lot of the Littles had on adorable T-shirts, a couple had on brightly colored overalls, and one even had a princess dress on, complete with tiara.

Something occurred to her then, though, and she turned to Tamsyn.

"So I get that you think I'm a Little."

Her BFF raised her brows in a way that said, *Excuse me, missy?* Maddie sighed.

"Fine. You recognized that I'm a Little. Is that better?"

"Yes. Proceed."

It shouldn't surprise her that her exacting-enough-to-be-an-actuary friend was so particular about semantics, but it sure was irritating sometimes.

"What I don't understand is what you're doing here."

Tamsyn blinked as if unprepared for the question then regained her composure. "Would you have come if I didn't drag you here?"

"No. But—"

Her would-be interrogation was interrupted by a man strolling over to where everyone was gathered and clapping his hands together.

"Good morning, everyone. I'm Travis, one of the stable heands here at Rawhide. You Littles can call me *Mister Travis* or *Sir*. We're going to have a lot of fun today, but it's also important that we all be safe, so I need you to listen very carefully and follow directions. Are we understood?"

"Yes, Mister Travis," the Littles chorused.

CHAPTER 4

If you would've told sixteen-year-old Reid Phillips that someday he would voluntarily shine tack, he would've called you a liar. It'd been one of his least favorite chores, along with mucking out stalls, because it was so fucking boring.

Now that he was thirty-eight, he wouldn't claim it had gotten all that much more interesting—it was still repetitive, fiddly, and time-consuming—but it had turned from a godforsaken chore to a meditative act. And a satisfying one at that.

It was soothing to sit in a corner of the tack room with Arlo—a young and quiet but hard-working guy Travis had introduced him to—and not say much while he polished brass fittings and the stable hand massaged leather balm into bridles and saddles.

The barn wasn't exactly what he'd describe as quiet—some horse or another was usually stomping, whinnying, or nickering; stable hands were joking around, talking about what else needed to be done or asking someone to lend a

A MEMORABLE LITTLE MEMORIAL DAY

hand; and, of course, here there were guests wandering in and out of the stables and around the riding rings, as well as people getting ready to go out on trail rides. But there was a lack of mechanical objects—no power tools, no grinding metal, no synthetic smells—and the only motors running were off in the distance.

Not that he'd ever give up working at Mason's to go back to toiling on his family's ranch, but now the surroundings felt easy, like a respite, instead of having him on edge. It was a nice change.

Nicer still to be able to set down the bridle he'd been working on, stretch out his shoulders and back, and tell Arlo he was going to take a walk. That was the thing, wasn't it? If something was your choice instead of something you were forced into, it was all the easier to deal with the unpleasantries or the challenges that went along with anything that had to do with living.

It was a good day to amble around: warm but not hot, and the dew on the grass had already evaporated. Not that his boots would be the worse for wear from a little water.

There were a few people riding in the rings, and in the one he was walking by, there was a bunch of Littles having a group lesson. Most of them were standing on the far side of the ring near the entry gate, a sea of black helmets and brightly colored clothes. He hadn't spent a ton of time with Littles, but he'd enjoyed the time he'd spent with Little girls. Not enough to stick around, clearly, but there was something about the dynamic that called to him. Maybe he'd take Fitz's advice and make more effort to meet some of the other guests—particularly the women—instead of hiding out in the stables. Maybe.

Reid was about to circle on back to the barn when there

was a commotion behind him. Littles shrieking, horses whinnying, lower voices trying to keep everyone calm. Must've been something happening in the ring, although he knew the Ranch was real careful with which horses the Littles were allowed to ride. Mild mannered, well trained, unflappable. Must've been something pretty big to be causing such a ruckus. He wasn't one to stick his nose where it didn't belong, but he also knew his way around horses, and if they needed a hand—

Reid heard the scream and was on the move before a sickening thud followed.

He vaulted over the fence to the ring and sprinted to where a woman was crumpled on the ground, black helmet still on and no bones at awkward angles that he could see, but shit.

The horse she'd been on was prancing in an agitated way, but at least it was headed away from them, so he wasn't concerned about being trampled. Especially when he saw one of the ranch hands snag the horse's bridle.

Which was when he saw the reason the horse had likely spooked and reared, throwing what he assumed was an inexperienced rider. Looked like the remains of a big snake —likely a gopher snake from the coloring—that the horse had brought its front hooves down on.

It only took a couple seconds for his brain to gather and process that information, and then he was scanning the woman on the ground for injuries. No blood, she was moving and breathing, and she made a soft, pained whimper. Probably more scared than hurt—horses were big animals, and it wasn't fun to take a tumble. He imagined it would be even more frightening if you were a slight, bird-boned thing and in the Little headspace. Poor thing.

A MEMORABLE LITTLE MEMORIAL DAY

* * *

"I'm fine," she told Tamsyn as her cheeks burned. It was bad enough that she'd fallen off a horse, even worse that she had half a dozen people standing over her with concern etched on their faces.

Someone had helped her sit up, but she was still on her butt in the dirt. If only she could melt and seep into the soil or maybe crumble into dust and get blown away on the breeze.

Her heart was still racing from the adrenaline that flooded her system when Star reared up and Maddie hadn't been able to hold on. It had all happened so fast she couldn't even say exactly what had gone wrong. Mostly that the previously very sweet horse had gotten worked up suddenly, stomping and nickering before making an ugly sound that had chilled her to the bone, and then she'd been flying through the air, and then... Owie. Big owie.

Pain had shot through her elbow like the least funny thing to ever happen to her funny bone, then the rest of her had hit the dirt. She'd had the wind knocked out of her, and it had been really unpleasant, but nothing felt broken. Except maybe her pride.

"You sure? Looked like a nasty spill, and it's no trouble to call the doc to look you over," Travis assured her.

It was definitely trouble. For her, for everyone else who was waiting their turn, for all the staff members who'd stopped what they were doing to stare at her. The only thing she wanted was to get out of here and hide in her room for the rest of the week. This was a bad idea, and she never should've let Tamsyn talk her into it.

Her hands shook as she took off the borrowed helmet,

and she tried to ignore how rattled and punchy she felt. She'd go lie down for a while and then get in the shower to wash away the dirt and hopefully some of the mortification would go with it. If only.

"Yes, I'm sure," she told the ranch hand. "I was just scared, but I'm not hurt. See?"

She hopped to her feet to prove she could and dusted off her jeans, hoping the Littles who were standing by would see she was 100 percent fine and they shouldn't be in such a tizzy. Their freaking out was only making things worse. But she really was okay. Nothing to see here, and she wished people would stop fussing. Okay, her elbow smarted, and she'd probably have a bruise there, but otherwise she felt fine. Totally fine. Absolutely, completely, and utterly fine.

Until cold rushed through her body where her veins ought to have been, and the ring started to spin around her before everything went black.

* * *

REID WAS glad he'd been standing at the woman's back when she jumped up from the dusty ground. He'd seen a lot of people thrown from a lot of horses, as well as having been thrown by a good few himself, and he knew the adrenaline rush could mask a lot of pain from injuries and make you feel invincible when you were anything but. He wasn't at all surprised when the brunette went from mortified but perky to passing out.

At least she wasn't going to hit the dirt because he caught her neatly and then hefted her body into his arms. She was not only petite but felt even lighter than she looked. Like a bird who'd smacked into glass and needed a second to come to.

"Unless you want to call a bus, I'll take her on up to the infirmary," he told Jagger, who'd rushed out from the barn when he'd heard the commotion.

The man, to his credit, looked as though he wanted to argue about that. For as much as he might like Reid—and Reid fancied they'd formed an amiable respect since yesterday—Reid wasn't an employee of the Ranch, wasn't even a frequent guest. But Reid knew Jagger was also a sensible sort, like he was. Most people he'd known to work on ranches were.

"You've got your hands full with calming Star and the other horses, disposing of the snake, and getting this lot in order," he said, gesturing to the Littles who were all in a tizzy with a lift of his chin. "I can take care of..."

Jesus, he didn't even know this woman's name.

"Maddie. Her name's Maddie. And you're not taking her anywhere without me. I'm Tamsyn, and we're here together."

Together together? Reid wanted to ask, but that wasn't important.

"Alright," Jagger agreed, still looking a little skeptical but also like a man with a job to do. "Here's Arlo now with the golf cart. Y'all head up to see Nurse Mac and have her radio me when you get there. She can call Doc Carter if we can't take care of Maddie here. I gotta—"

He tossed a thumb in the direction of the Littles who still seemed to be freaking out pretty good, despite Travis doing his best to settle them down. But Reid was sure the two steady men would be able to calm them, maybe get some of them to take a ride even after what they'd seen.

Reid wasn't going to worry about those Littles, though;

the one in his arms was enough. Trailed by her friend, he made his way to where Arlo had parked the cart. Tamsyn took the seat next to the hand, and Reid settled onto the bench in the back with Maddie.

"You got her, Reid?" the stable hand asked over his shoulder.

"Yep. Deadweight but still light as a feather," he assured his new friend before Arlo put the cart in gear.

On the way to the main lodge, Reid had a chance to study the woman in his lap. Real pretty in a girl-next-door kind of way, braided pigtails, long lashes fanning over her cheeks, and a mouth that was begging to be kissed.

You fucking horndog, he heard Fitz say in his head. *Can you at least wait for her to wake up before you start perving on her?*

As if she'd heard his friend's disgusted comment, the woman's lashes fluttered and then her eyes flew open, revealing the clearest blue irises he'd ever seen. Brighter than his own pale blues, her eyes made him feel like he was looking at the sky.

Reid felt the woman's muscles tense like she was about to put up a fight. Falling off the back of a golf cart wasn't going to help anything, and she was already going to be plenty sore.

"Hey, now, darlin'. Take it easy. You passed out after you got thrown. We're bringing you up to the infirmary to get checked out. Your friend's in the front."

"You don't need to do that. I'm fine. I—"

Reid was about to tell her she was clearly not fine because she'd dropped to the ground like a sack of potatoes, but it turned out he didn't have to. In her effort to sit up, Maddie bumped her elbow against the seat, and she made the most pitiful noise, followed by a pained little "ow."

"See now? You got roughed up when you fell, and that's probably not the only thing you hurt. So just stay still, and we'll get you looked over right quick."

CHAPTER 5

Maddie perched on the edge of the exam table feeling abashed. So humiliating. Especially because the man who had carried her in here was so handsome. Like a cowboy who'd ambled off the cover of a romance novel.

And he was still here. Why? Surely he had something cowboy-y to do, like ride a bull or rope a steer or sing "Home on the Range." Feed his hound dog or clean his gun. Organize his Stetson collection. Something, anything, that would get him out of here.

Alas, the man didn't seem to be going anywhere. His ice-blue gaze was laser focused on her while Nurse Mac looked her over, and she couldn't help but notice his ropy, tanned forearms that were bared by the rolled up sleeves of his Western-style shirt. Honestly, didn't the man have a rodeo or a hoedown to get to?

"Well, Miss Maddie," said Nurse Mac, "it looks to me like you're going to have a pretty sore and swollen arm for a few days and probably some bruises elsewhere, but other than that, you should be fine. I do want you to take it easy for the rest of the day at least—get some ice on that arm to keep the swelling down and maybe take a nap. You'll probably feel shaken up and sore for a while, and that's to be expected. But if your hand gets numb or anything gets worse, you call me right away."

"Yes, ma'am," Maddie conceded, hoping she could get the heck out of this infirmary and on with her business. Her business being to crawl under some blankets and never show her face at the Ranch until she was ready to head to the airport and back to Penshaw.

She smiled at Tamsyn, feeling sheepish and mortified. "Sorry I messed up your plans."

"You didn't mess anything up," Tamsyn insisted. "This is just an excuse for us to chill out, maybe watch a movie. Oh, I can grab some snacks from the store, and we'll have some noms while we hang. It'll be great."

Maddie doubted it would be great. "You should go to the painting class like you planned to. I promise you won't miss anything exciting."

"Not a chance. This is all about me and you, silly."

She could argue more, but there was no way she could out-stubborn Tamsyn on this one. Or pretty much anything. Not that Maddie couldn't dig her heels in, but she had nothing on her friend.

"Fine. Let's go."

She thanked Nurse Mac and hopped down from the table, wincing when the movement jarred her sore arm. Owie, owie, ow.

Cradling her swelling elbow with her other hand, Maddie headed out of the infirmary with Tamsyn by her side and dipped her head to the man who was still standing by the door like he was her bodyguard or some nonsense.

"Thank you," she muttered, not wanting to be rude but not even able to look at him. He was too gorgeous, and she was way too embarrassed.

"I'll walk you to your room," he said, and Maddie could appreciate for the first time his whisky-like voice. Smooth but strong, and you'd best watch out because that stuff could wreck a girl before she knew which way was up. Trouble, that's what this man was. Or would be if she had any interest in him.

"Oh, you don't need to do that. I'm fine."

"Would you quit saying that, please? I don't think girls who get thrown from a horse and then pass out should be able to say they're fine for at least twenty-four hours. You don't seem all that steady on your feet. Can't have you collapsing in the hallway."

Ugh, she was tired and achy, and she wanted to go lie down, not argue with some too-good-looking cowboy with a hero complex.

"I appreciate the offer," she gritted out between her teeth, "but my friend will walk with me. We'll be fine."

"Or I could get snacks while Reid walks you back to our room," Tamsyn piped up from her side, and Maddie shot her a death glare. "It was Reid, wasn't it?"

"Yes, ma'am. Reid Phillips at your service."

Maddie got the feeling that Mr. Reid Phillips wasn't at anyone's service no matter what he said, but she was also feeling too run-down to fight what she knew would end up being a losing battle.

"Fine."

* * *

A MEMORABLE LITTLE MEMORIAL DAY

MADDIE WAS silent as he walked her to her room. That was fine with him—people talked too much.

Or it would've been fine if he didn't have the urge to pepper her with a hundred questions. Like where was she from, what was she doing here, was she a Little? Because she'd been at the Littles' riding lesson, but she wasn't staying in the Littles' dorms, so maybe not. She sure hadn't been acting like a Little, at least not with him or with Nurse Mac. But maybe Tamsyn, the woman who'd said they were here together, was her Mommy? Except Maddie had called Tamsyn her friend, so maybe not. The uncertainty was making him twitchy.

It was far too soon that they reached a door Maddie gestured to with her thumb.

"That's me. Thanks for...escorting me here," she said, although she sounded more annoyed than grateful. "As you can see, I haven't passed out, and my arm hasn't fallen off, so I think you can go."

"I don't think so. I'll get you settled, and then I'll leave."

"I'm fi—"

Reid usually kept the Daddy in him under wraps. He didn't want to come across as condescending when he talked to women at the garage, and while some women were into his take-charge attitude in bed, it took him a bit to exert his dominance outside the bedroom. Long enough that with his usual one-night stands or a few weeks of casual dating the protectiveness and possessiveness and the caretaking didn't generally show up at all.

But there was something about Maddie that had him giving her his sternest Daddy glare when they'd only just met. One that hopefully told her there was no way he was leaving without seeing her tucked under a blanket on the couch with a glass of water and her phone—with his number entered into the contacts—nearby.

And if he had to tell her one more time that she wasn't fine, well... If she were his, she'd be going over his knee for arguing with Daddy.

But she wasn't, so he merely stood there and hoped his toppy gaze would convince her to give in. He'd learned to be patient and stubborn from working with livestock, and there was no way this girl was going to outlast him. Which she seemed to realize a minute into their standoff.

"You aren't going to leave, are you?"

"Not until I'm sure you're safe and as comfortable as possible."

"And if I don't unlock my room?"

"Then we'll stand in the hallway until Tamsyn gets back. No skin off my nose. But you look like a stiff breeze could knock you over, so maybe you want to rethink that."

The truth was that he itched to scoop her up in his arms, carry her over the threshold, and either tuck her into bed so she could get some rest or cuddle her in his lap and fuss over her, but neither of those things was going to happen. He'd have to settle for getting her off her feet with an ice pack on her arm as soon as possible. Tenderness for her was bubbling up inside of him, and while it wasn't familiar, he didn't feel the urge to fight it either.

Maddie pouted, and it made him want to swat her backside or maybe grip her jaw and give her a warning about having good manners. He didn't think she was bratty, but... there was something going on that he couldn't quite puzzle out.

Maddie wasn't vibrantly and enthusiastically Little like a lot of the Littles he'd seen cavorting around the Ranch, but he was almost certain she was in fact Little. Maybe in denial about it? Some people were. Or maybe she knew but didn't like that about herself and kept it under wraps? A stealth Little, if you will, and the thought had him swallowing a laugh.

After a few more beats, Maddie sighed, and some of the stubborn melted from her soft features.

"I am pretty tired," she admitted. "And I feel kinda...I don't know. Shaky?"

She held up a hand and looked at it as if it weren't connected to her body. Poor thing was trembling.

"That's 'cause you're all aquiver, darlin'," he told her, steadied her hand, and took the key card from it. "Getting tossed off a horse can make all the chemicals in your body go haywire. You'll feel steadier soon."

He unlocked the door and steered her through it with a hand at the small of her back. The urge to sweep her off her feet was almost unbearable as she shuffled into the room, but Maddie had made it clear she was barely tolerating his presence as things were. She'd probably clock him good if he tried to pick her up. Which, given her size, probably wouldn't hurt too bad—maybe get him a shiner, if that— but really, he didn't want her to hurt *herself*. The girl didn't exactly look like she knew how to throw a punch.

* * *

THAT UNSTEADY, exhausted feeling was hitting her pretty hard, and Maddie didn't have the strength to shoo Reid away. It was also possible that a teeny tiny part of her was enjoying his attention.

His size could have been intimidating, especially now

that they were alone, but he didn't scare her. Not with the soft twang of his voice and the way his palm and fingertips rested low on her back—enough pressure to let her feel supported and know he was there if she needed him but not enough to feel pushy.

She let him guide her over to the couch and tried not to plop down too hard so as not to jostle her arm. A pained groan escaped her anyway because it seemed like everything was starting to hurt. All she wanted to do was nestle into some blankets and feel sorry for herself.

The urge to curl up was strong, but she still had her boots on, and she wasn't so far gone that she'd put shoes on the furniture. But bending down to take them off seemed almost as impossible as winning the Kentucky Derby after her little performance.

She was equally relieved and horrified when Reid knelt in front of her and started to untie her boots as though he'd read her mind. If she were by herself, she would've had to wait for Tamsyn to get back and help her, but did her feet smell? She couldn't bear to ask, so she covered her flushing face with her hands while he undid her boots and gently slipped them off before sliding his big hands behind her ankles and helping her turn to sit sideways on the big comfy couch.

"There you go, Maddie-girl. Bet it feels good to get your feet up. Let's get you a blanket since you're still shivering, and then I'll see about some ice for that arm of yours."

Usually men being so familiar with her would make her prickly, and she did resent Reid a little for calling her *darlin'* and *Maddie-girl*. But mostly because it felt nice. Touched something deep inside that made her want to let all her tears out and climb into his lap so he could cuddle and comfort her. Soothe her pain and her embarrassment.

That, however, was ridiculous, and she would not be giving in to those foolish urges that had come out of nowhere. Maybe she ought to call Nurse Mac since she'd clearly suffered a concussion or some other brain damage. Or maybe she would just let Reid take the blanket from the foot of the bed and tuck it around her before he went off to rummage in the little kitchenette.

The man was back a minute later with a few ice cubes wrapped in a damp kitchen towel and a glass of water with a bright blue bendy straw. He parked himself on the coffee table in front of her, and the denim of his jeans hugged his thick thighs, which she tried not to notice...unsuccessfully.

Reid was gentle when he arranged her arm to set the ice on it, and then he held the glass up to her. He frowned when she took the water from him, but he didn't argue. The bendy straw had been a thoughtful touch so she didn't have to sit up fully to drink.

She took a few sips and was about to hand it back to him when he shook his head. "Drink a little more. Water's good for pretty much anything that ails you."

It was annoying that her body complied without her brain's permission, but that was probably just the disjointed shakiness she was feeling. Not anything to do with his easy confidence and the stern set of his jaw.

"Anything else I can get you? Do for you?" he asked.

A big part of her wanted to reply tartly that he'd done quite enough. But that would be rude and uncalled for. Reid had only been kind and attentive, and it wouldn't be fair to respond with cheek, even if she was feeling crabby and vulnerable. Besides, there was one thing she desperately wanted.

"Would you—"

Ugh, no, she couldn't. Could not ask this very grown,

wildly handsome, and slightly gruff man for what she really wanted. But Reid cocked a brow and his ice-blue eyes seemed to bore into her.

"Yes. Just tell me what you need."

It didn't feel like he was exaggerating, not in the least. Maddie suspected that if she asked for a star from the sky, he'd reach up and grab one for her, set it in the palms of her hands. The mix of his firmness and tenderness was going to turn her inside out.

"There's a manatee on the bed," she whispered, feeling ridiculous.

Before she could explain that it wasn't an actual manatee but a stuffed toy and her name was Cleopatra because four-year-old Maddie had thought she was so beautiful, Reid was on his feet, striding over to the big bed and coming back with her beloved stuffie. She never went anywhere without Cleopatra, but mostly she never went anywhere.

Reid tucked the well-loved manatee under the blanket so only her grey snout and beady black eyes poked out, and Maddie cuddled her closer with her good arm. Cleopatra was the perfect size to hug and always made her feel better.

Luckily, before she could say or do anything else silly, Tamsyn bustled back into the room bearing not bags from the gift shop but wicker picnic baskets.

"Somehow Chef Connor heard about what happened—"

Oh no. Of course he had. Gossip probably spread like wildfire in a place like the Ranch, and she was going to be known as that foolish girl who fell off a horse for the rest of their stay. Maybe they should just leave now.

"—and wouldn't hear of me buying snacks from the gift shop. He insisted on making up some sandwiches and put in some fruit and nuts since healthy food will make you feel better faster. But I also saw him put in a couple bowls of chocolate mousse and some popcorn."

She set that basket on the coffee table next to Reid and then held up the other one.

"This one's from Nurse Mac. It has some freezy packs for your arm, although it looks like Reid's already taken care of that," she said approvingly, and Maddie had to roll her eyes.

Apparently Tamsyn had been saving all her meddling for this trip. At least she'd only have to suffer through her friend trying to throw her toward any vaguely Daddy-shaped person nearby for the next week.

"Also your next dose of pain meds and instructions for them and when to ice your arm. I'd ask if you need anything else, but..."

"I'm fine," Maddie said, cheeks heating as she caught Reid's glare from the corner of her eye. He looked as though he wanted to take her over his knee, and despite being in rough shape, she felt a pulse of want.

Tamsyn must've missed Reid's glower because she'd started unpacking the food picnic basket.

"Whoa. I think Chef Connor must've packed enough food to feed an army. Are you hungry, Reid? You should stay. We're not going to eat all this."

If eyeball daggers could kill, Tamsyn would be bleeding out on the floor. Seriously, what had happened that her bestie had gone from pretty darn chill to an intrusive busybody?

Reid opened his mouth to reply, and in that moment, Maddie didn't honestly know if she wanted him to stay or go. She really must've shaken up her brain pretty good in the fall because she'd never been boy crazy, but after Josh she'd steered clear of men almost altogether. Thankfully, she was saved by the bell. Or rather Reid's phone ringing from his pocket.

The man held up a finger and dug it out before answering with an easy, "This is Phillips."

CHAPTER 6

Ten minutes later, Reid found himself sitting across a very large desk from the owner of the Ranch, Derek Hawkins himself. He was a big man, the kind of guy who could be a doting if strict Daddy to his Little girl but also a fierce Papa Bear if anyone messed with his people. Reid could appreciate that.

He hadn't wanted to leave Maddie when he'd been summoned, but he also didn't feel as though he had much of a choice. Not with the chipper but no-nonsense tone of Derek's receptionist, Erika. And then he'd tried to ignore the sting of Maddie looking relieved when he'd said he had to go.

What was the big deal? She'd made it clear she didn't want him around; it shouldn't have surprised him that she was glad to see the back of him. But he thought she'd warmed to him at least a little. She'd trusted him enough to get her stuffie, and that wasn't a small thing for a Little girl.

In too much of a hurry to convince Maddie to put his number in her phone, he'd scribbled it on the instructions Nurse Mac had provided and told the girls he was sure the

Ranch staff would be more than accommodating but if they needed anything, they should feel free to call him too.

Tamsyn had smiled sweetly and warmly expressed her gratitude, while Maddie muttered a reluctant thanks, but it wasn't the gushing woman with the dirty-blond hair he'd found himself thinking of as he strode down the hallway; it was the guarded brunette.

"You rang?" he joked with Derek after they'd shaken hands and set themselves down in the chairs.

"I did. Are you enjoying your stay so far?"

That was obviously not what Derek had called him in here for, and Reid would much rather be back with Maddie making sure she ate something and took it easy, but he could be pleasant.

"Sure am. You've got a nice place here. Food's good, staff is friendly, horses are well cared for. But I don't think you personally invite every guest to your office to see how we're doing."

"I would if I had the time," Derek mused, "but you're correct. I actually had a proposition for you."

A proposition? From the owner of the Ranch? Maybe he'd heard Reid had been hanging around the stables and was going to offer him a job as a ranch hand? Not that he'd take it since he was happy at Mason's, but he could think of worse things than working with Travis and Jagger and Arlo and hanging around here. At least for a little while, that was —he'd never be able to work on a ranch full-time ever again.

"I'm listening."

"It's actually regarding Maddie Arsenault."

Now he was listening harder. What about Maddie?

The corner of Derek's mouth twitched, probably noticing the way Reid had sat straighter in his chair.

"She's a bit of an unusual guest for us, here at her friend's behest. Usually we'd insist unaccompanied Littles stay in the Littles' dorms," Derek said, steepling his fingers as his elbows rested on the desk. "But Miss Yates was concerned Miss Arsenault might refuse to stay if pushed to fully participate as a Little."

Yeah, he could see that. Both that Maddie did seem to be a Little but also that she might tell anyone who insisted she was to fuck off. Although probably with nicer language even if it was the same sentiment.

"So," the Ranch owner continued, "we've made an exception and allowed the girls to stay in a regular guest suite and given them more latitude than we'd usually permit Littles. Mostly because Miss Yates identifies as a Middle and agreed to act as a babysitter for Miss Arsenault."

Reid was glad for the information—it helped him piece together more of Maddie and Tamsyn's relationship and what their deal was with being here—but he wasn't sure why Derek was sharing all this stuff with him. Wasn't sure Maddie would appreciate it either.

"Okay. Not sure what this has to do with me, though."

"Excellent question. Generally, we'd pair a guest with a staff member during their stay if they weren't going to be residing in the Littles' dorm. Their assigned Big would escort them to and from activities, that sort of thing. But based on what I've heard from Jagger and Travis and Nurse Mac, it sounded like there's a connection of sorts between you and Miss Arsenault."

Reid fought the urge to shove his hands in his pockets. Yeah, Derek was older and ran this whole show, but they were both men, Bigs, peers. Wasn't like he was being called to the principal's office.

"Of sorts," he agreed. "I didn't mean to step on any

toes, and I'm sure your staff could've handled it. I'm just not the kind of man who can see a hand wouldn't go amiss and not offer one."

"I understand, being that kind of man myself."

Reid had hoped the older man would.

"So, unless you have reason to refuse, I'd like to assign you to be Miss Arsenault's Daddy for the length of her stay."

Damn. That was not what he'd been expecting when he'd gotten the call that Derek wanted to see him in his office.

"If you're not prepared to take on that responsibility, I'll find someone else to do it. Nothing worse than a Little girl feeling unwanted or like a burden because the Big who's supposed to be minding her doesn't want the job. Especially if she's not real comfortable in her skin. Those ill-at-ease Littles are likely to use that as proof they don't deserve to be Little or that there's something wrong with them instead of assigning the blame where it belongs."

Reid could see that. From the time he'd spent with Littles, he'd gotten the impression that even if they were sturdy and resilient, they could also be real sensitive and easily bruised—emotionally anyway.

"I'd be happy to look after Maddie, but only if she'll have me. I like her just fine"—that was an understatement if there ever was one—"but I'm not sure she feels the same about me."

"You leave that up to me," Derek said, settling his palms on the desk as if the matter were a done deal.

Did the rancher know something he didn't? Why was he so certain Maddie would agree to let him be her Daddy for the week when *he* was pretty damn unsure how the woman felt about him?

But he wasn't going to say no to having an official reason to check in on Maddie, spend some more time with her, fuss over her. Maybe get his hands on her. He'd been envious of her manatee as she'd snuggled the stuffie close, and how sad was that? Jealous of a stuffed animal. Better not spill that to Fitz, or he'd never hear the end of it.

"Oh, and one last thing before I speak with Maddie. We run a tight ship here at the Ranch. I'll be keeping a close eye on you, and if you harm a single hair on that Little girl's head, I won't hesitate to give you the boot. You'll be blacklisted from here and anywhere I have pull. I've also got the local LEOs on speed dial and we're on real good terms. You get me?"

A shiver ran down Reid's spine. He didn't doubt for a second that Derek Hawkins took protecting the Littles under his purview very seriously. That man might have laugh lines around his eyes and a ready smile, but Reid could sense the steel in his soul behind that crisp white shirt and spit-shined bolo tie.

"Yes, sir."

CHAPTER 7

"What is wrong with you?"

Tamsyn looked at her like she was the one with three heads. Not fair. "I'm sorry, what's wrong with me? What's wrong with *you*?"

"Nothing's wrong with me. I am the same person I've always been. You, on the other hand, have turned into some matchmaking yenta."

"There you have it," her friend said. "I am reacting sensibly to this situation, and you are not."

"And what situation would that be?" Maddie demanded, regretting the words as soon as they were out of her mouth because Tamsyn was now grinning like the Cheshire cat. Maddie had never liked that mischievous and unpredictable feline.

"Reid Phillips is clearly quite enamored of you. And if you had any sense in your head, you would encourage his infatuation instead of acting like you're not interested."

"I'm not acting! I'm not interested!"

It was a good thing she'd been subjected to Tamsyn's withering glare many times over the years because otherwise she might've actually withered under her friend's stare.

"And why on god's green earth not? He's easy on the eyes and total Daddy material."

"Yes, he's good-looking. But I don't... I don't do that."

"You don't fuck hunky cowboys who look at you like you're a steak and they're starving?"

"Ew."

"You remember your promise?"

"Of course I do. Did I stab him in the eye? I did not."

Honestly, that seemed very generous to Maddie, but Tamsyn rolled her eyes and grumbled.

"I'm just not ready."

"It's been five years. When are you going to be ready?" her BFF demanded.

"Maybe never," she said softly and then turned her attention to Cleopatra. The manatee never gave her a hard time and was very quiet. Perhaps it was for the best that her stuffie was going to be her new best friend after Tamsyn left for her fancy new life in Clover City.

"You're impossible. Now stop arguing with me and eat your sandwiches."

Chef Connor had cut them up into quarters so it was easy to pick up in one hand and not stuffed them too full, so nothing came spilling out.

Maddie took a bite, and while she might've still felt pretty out of sorts, she was with it enough to appreciate how good the sandwich was. Crusty sourdough bread with a filling of creamy egg salad and the crisp coolness of cucumber slices.

"This is so good," she told Tamsyn, mouth still full.

"Right?"

"Are you having the egg salad?"

"No, I thought I'd save those for you. I've got roast beef and Boursin."

Ooo, that sounded good too. "Want to trade a quarter?"

They swapped a segment, and Maddie was about to sink her teeth into another sandwich quarter when there was a knock at the door.

Tamsyn hopped up to answer it, and Maddie craned her neck to see who her friend was letting in. She almost choked on her sandwich when she saw it was Master Derek, Sadie's husband. He seemed even bigger in person than he did in the pictures she'd seen, and that was pretty big.

"Sorry to interrupt your lunch, ladies. Glad to see Chef Connor rustled up some chow for you girls. You just call the front desk if you need anything else."

"Pretty sure we're going to be stuffed by the time we've eaten half of this," Tamsyn told him and then gestured him to the seating area where Maddie was ensconced on the couch. "Did you want to come in, sit down?"

"I will, thank you."

The large man came over and sat in the chair Tamsyn hadn't been occupying.

"How are you feeling, Maddie? I heard you took a spill down at the stables earlier."

His face bore only concern, but Maddie was mortified anyway. Yep, just as she'd feared. Everyone was going to hear about her horse mishap.

She opened her mouth to tell him she was fine, but the stern look in his eyes said she'd best only tell him the truth. What was with all the bossy pants men around here?

"A little shaken up and the arm I fell on hurts, but other than that, I'm okay."

"Glad to hear it. It can be scary to get thrown from a

horse. They're big, powerful animals. Ours are very well trained, but even the most mild-mannered, easygoing horse can get spooked by a snake."

Yeah, she could understand that. She wasn't a huge fan of snakes herself. "Oh, I don't blame Star or Mister Travis or anyone else. It was an accident."

"Then I hope you're not blaming yourself either," he told her with a meaningful look.

"No, Sir," she said, although part of her had been.

"That's good. The only one at fault was that darn sneaky snake."

She couldn't help the corner of her mouth turning up at his silliness. Master Derek didn't strike her as the silly type, but he did seem like a man who genuinely cared about his guests, particularly the Littles.

"Now, I did come here to look in on you, but that wasn't the only thing I wanted to talk to you about."

"Okay?"

"You know the Ranch is a very special place where it's safe for people to explore parts of themselves they can't in the real world, right?"

"Yes, Sir."

"We made some exceptions for you and Tamsyn because she didn't think you were quite ready to full-on explore your Little side. But the thing is, you're only here for a week, and I don't want you missing out."

Maddie's heart thumped in her chest, and she wasn't certain if it was excitement or dread. Maybe both. What did Master Derek mean?

"I'm not going to insist you move into the Littles' dorm or sign up for school. I can understand how that might feel overwhelming, and I don't want to push you too hard, too fast. However..."

Oh no. What was he going to insist on? She'd only ever let herself be truly Little with Josh, and she didn't know that she was prepared to let anyone else see that unvarnished part of her. Even Tamsyn. It felt next to impossible that she could ever be that open again.

"I do think it's important for you to try. I want you to at least enjoy some of the comfort that comes with being Little. Part of what we do here sometimes when we have unaccompanied Littles is pair them up with a caregiver. I hadn't before you arrived because I didn't feel like I had anyone on staff who would be a good fit. But I'm going to now."

"Who?"

She hadn't met all that many people who worked here, and she thought all the ones she had met were partnered, if not married. Maybe it would be strictly platonic because some Littles and Bigs were. Or maybe some staff members were polyamorous or ethically nonmonogamous? People certainly had all sorts of relationship structures that made them happy. Or maybe Master Derek had someone on staff who was really great with clumsy Littles? Maybe they had a bubble wrap fetish? This day just kept getting worse.

"It's a little unconventional"—thank goodness Master Derek had the good grace to give her a small smile that said he was aware his entire operation was more than just a tad unconventional—"but I'm going to pair you with another guest."

Another— Oh no. No no no no no. He couldn't. He wouldn't. But Maddie knew exactly whose name was going to come out of Master Derek's mouth when he spoke next, and she wasn't wrong.

"For the next week, Reid Phillips is going to be your Daddy."

CHAPTER 8

Maddie was thankful Master Derek had given her the rest of the day to recover from her fall, but the next morning, it didn't seem like it had been long enough. Especially when he called to say she should be dressed and ready for Reid to come by at nine. "And don't you forget to eat breakfast, little girl," he'd tacked on.

It had taken Tamsyn a while to talk her into agreeing to Reid being her Daddy for the week. In the end, she'd acquiesced. Partly because she wanted to make Tamsyn and Master Derek happy, but also because they assured her that if she was truly unhappy, she could change her mind at any time.

She had fretted over what to wear for maybe half an hour before Tamsyn shoved some jeans and a sunny yellow-and-white ruched gingham shirt with puffy sleeves at her. Why did she care anyway? It wasn't like she wanted to impress Reid.

If she had it in her, she'd just refuse. Although she suspected if she did, she would simply end up with a butt that was as sore and bruised as her arm from Master

Derek's paddle. Plus, she'd never been a disobedient Little. Or even much of a brat. So grudging cooperation it was.

"Put this on and I'll do your hair."

Maddie supposed she could've argued with her bestie, but what was the point? She didn't have a better idea.

It did calm her nerves some to have Tamsyn brush her hair and then fashion it into two French-braided pigtails and help her get her shoes on—brown booties with a zipper on the inside. She knew she looked younger than even her twenty-four years in this outfit, and it certainly made her feel younger. Was Reid going to like that or nah? Ugh, why had Master Derek taken a special interest in her? She wished she'd never fallen off that darn horse. No, that wasn't fair to Star. Poor horsey had been as scared as she was.

Which was only slightly more terrified than Maddie was when there was a knock at her door. Tamsyn practically shoved her toward the entrance to their room, and when Maddie returned the push with a scowl, Tamsyn hissed at her, "You better be careful, or your face will stick like that!"

This had been the worst idea in the history of ideas, and she wished she'd left when she'd figured out what Tamsyn had done. But she hadn't, so now here she was with a sore arm and greeting the gorgeous man who'd been assigned to be her Daddy for the next week. What the heck?

Maddie tried to smile when she opened the door, but she suspected it turned out more like a grimace. Not like the wide grin Reid beamed down on her as though he were the sun. A very handsome, cowboy-shaped sun.

"Morning, Maddie."

"Good morning."

"You had your breakfast?"

"Yes." As if she'd disobey Master Derek. He'd probably put her over his knee if she did.

A line formed between Reid's dark brows.

"I know this is all a little funny—it is for me too—but since I'm your Daddy for the rest of the week, I think you ought to address me with some respect."

Maddie's stomach plummeted, and she thought she might be sick. She couldn't—

"Hey, darlin'," Reid said, resting a hand on her shoulder. "No need to look like you saw another snake. *Daddy*'s a lot to ask, I know that. How about we start with *Sir*?"

She didn't think Reid *did* know how much it would be asking to call him *Daddy*, but she did appreciate that he wasn't going to be a hard-ass about it. His assurances let her take a breath and find her head.

She could do *Sir*. It might even be nice. It meant respect, yes, but it also meant he was taking on responsibility for her. She liked that feeling of being held in someone's hands, of someone looking after her. Tamsyn did some, but it wasn't the same.

"Yes, Sir," she tried. The big smile she got from the Montana-sized cowboy made her feel warm inside, and she had to remind herself this was just for a few days.

"There you go. That's a good girl."

Her pleasure intensified but so did her fear. She couldn't let herself feel this way again. If she was even capable, and she didn't think she was. Her attraction to Reid was a brief pulse of lust and nothing more. As Tamsyn had said, he was easy on the eyes. It was only natural for her to acknowledge that.

"So, um, what do we do now?"

There was the sound of skin slapping skin behind her, and she just knew it was Tamsyn face-palming at her scintillating conversational skills. Whatever, this definitely hadn't been her idea, so everyone could just deal with her being awkward.

"You know what you gotta do when you fall off a horse?"

"Never go near a horse again?" she offered, and Reid laughed.

"No, darlin'. You gotta get back on."

Of course, she'd heard the expression before, but she'd never tried to apply it to an actual horse.

"I don't think that's a good idea."

"How come?"

"Because my health insurance sucks. What if I got lucky last time? What if I get thrown again and really hurt myself? What if—"

"My goodness you've got a busy brain, little girl," Reid said, interrupting her fretting with his words and with his big hands chafing her biceps. His voice was warm and felt like it swirled around her somehow. Like when she was a kid and her dad would let her put the cream in his coffee. Reid was maybe teasing her, but it didn't feel unkind. Or condescending.

Maddie didn't bother to agree—what was the point?

"Okay, here's what we're going to do."

"We?"

Outside of Tamsyn, she didn't often find herself part of a *we*.

"Yes, we. You came here to ride a horse, right?"

"Among other things, apparently," she conceded, heat rushing to her cheeks. Her face burned hotter when Reid grinned in response. "But I did ride a horse, so mission accomplished."

"Oh, I don't think so. I'm not letting you leave here until you have a good experience with a horse."

"Why do you care?"

Reid shrugged. "I don't like seeing Little girls disappointed."

She shouldn't be disappointed that he hadn't singled her out, that he was obviously doing this because Master Derek had asked him to. Probably as a favor. Not because he actually liked her.

What would a man like Reid Phillips want with a foolish girl like her anyway? He was handsome and rugged and strong, and she was...silly. And weak. And scared. But that was just it, wasn't it? He didn't want her. Not really. Master Derek had paired them up because he felt sorry for her, and Reid was too much of a gentleman to say no.

"That's nice of you, but no thanks."

Reid's cool blue eyes narrowed, and Maddie felt hers widen in response.

"I'm not letting you off that easy, darlin'. You can either come with me to the stables holding my hand, or you can come with me to the stables over my shoulder with your bottom in the air. One way or another, we're gonna go see a horse."

He held out one of those rough hands, and Maddie's heart went into overdrive, pounding in her chest. He wouldn't. Would he? And if he did...

Shut up, she hissed at the voice in her head whispering that it might not be so bad, maybe even kind of fun, to get manhandled like that.

"You wouldn't," she said, crossing her arms over her chest and then wincing because her arm still hurt like the dickens.

Reid's dark brow arched, and somehow that tick of a

few small muscles made her pulse between her legs. "Try me."

Something in his tone said he wasn't kidding. And as much as the fantasy of him slinging her over his shoulder and carrying her off to have his way with her might make her wet, the reality of it would be beyond humiliating.

Ever so reluctantly, she slipped her hand into his and almost swooned when he smiled and said, "Good girl."

* * *

THERE WAS something easy about walking down to the stables with Maddie, even if he had to shorten his long stride so she wouldn't have to scurry to keep up with him. It wasn't a short walk, but they weren't in a hurry. As far as he was concerned, this could take all day and he wouldn't consider it wasted.

He'd informed Fitz over dinner last night about his new Daddy duties, and his friend had hidden his face up to his eyeballs behind the menu. But Reid had known that ginger bastard long enough to see the laughter and smugness in his eyes. Because Fitz was a first-rate, blue-ribbon asshole.

He needed to put Fitz out of his mind and instead pay attention to the beautiful girl he'd coerced into going down to the stables. She looked real sweet and soft in her jeans and a white-and-yellow top that hugged her slim curves.

"I thought we might get to know each other a bit since we'll be spending some time together this week," he said.

Not that he wanted to interrupt the peaceful quiet of a soft breeze that carried muted noises of Littles out on the playground from one direction and some barely distinguishable sounds of livestock from the other direction.

He really wasn't that much for small talk either, but he

did want Maddie to feel comfortable with him, know she could talk to him, count on him, trust him. Hopefully his invitation would make her start to believe that.

"Anything you want to ask me?" Reid prompted.

She had her hair in those fancy twin braids again, and he realized Tamsyn must've done them since there would be no way for Maddie to fix them with her arm aching the way it must. He could see the swelling and the bruising starting to come up even though she'd assured him she'd been icing as Nurse Mac had directed.

"Um...so many things," she said, looking up at him sheepishly, her cheeks turning a pretty shade of pink he didn't think had anything to do with the sun. "Sir."

Good lord, it got his blood running when she called him that.

"Well, I'll start with some basics, and then you can go from there. I'm thirty-eight, I live in Almandine, Montana, which is about four hours from here, and I'm a mechanic."

Maddie nodded as if filing away that information and then looked up at him through her lashes. "Is this your first time coming to the Ranch?"

"Sure is. This place has been nothing but surprises since we got here."

He felt the twitch of her hand in his when he'd said *we*, and he rushed to reassure her. "I'm here with a buddy of mine. We go way back, friends for almost half my lifetime. His name's Fitz, and I'm sure you'll meet him whether I want you to or not. That's a reflection on him, not on you. He's a real character but loyal as the day is long."

Maddie made a little humming sound. "Do you work on cars or bigger machinery or other stuff?"

"Mostly cars, although I've been known to fix up a tractor or a snow machine if needs must."

"And... And..."

"Go on, darlin'. You can ask me anything you like. Master Derek threw us into the deep end of the pool, but we may as well learn how to swim, right?"

He was proud to have gotten a huff of laughter out of the girl walking beside him.

"I was just wondering why you came here."

"Same reason I do anything else. Fitz made me."

Maddie giggled when he winked at her, and he relished the sound.

CHAPTER 9

"Hey, Arlo."

"Hey," the stable hand responded, looking flummoxed as he scratched behind an ear. "Y'all missed the last trail ride for the morning. They headed out twenty minutes ago."

"That's alright; we weren't really feeling up for that today anyway. You got any horses that stayed behind and we could say hi to?"

Reid tilted his head toward Maddie, who was rubbing her injured arm with the hand that wasn't clutching his and was no doubt looking a little terrified. Hopefully Arlo would remember Maddie from yesterday and would get the message.

After a beat, it did seem like he'd connected the dots—understanding lit his face as clear as if he'd been standing under a bare bulb that got switched on.

"Sure do. Peanut's not big enough to go out on the trail with his momma yet, and I'm sure he'd appreciate some visitors."

Arlo walked them through the stable, and Reid didn't

fail to notice the way Maddie clung to his side and flinched when any of the horses stamped or whinnied in their stalls.

"They're just saying hi," he assured her. "They're curious about you. But they're all secure in their stalls, so all they can do is poke their heads out."

Maddie looked up at him, skeptical as all hell, but nodded.

Finally, they reached the end of the building and stood in front of a stall labeled *Peanut*. Arlo let them in, and the little horse eyed them curiously.

"Hey, buddy," Arlo said, giving him some scritches behind the ears. "I brought you some friends."

Maddie hung back but peeked out at Peanut from behind Reid's arm. It was hard not to smile when you were near the little guy; he was cute as a button.

"Peanut's real friendly. He's used to getting petted and brushed and fed by all the Littles. Travis's wife even snuck him into the Littles' wing when she was living there before they got married."

Wow. Reid had heard rumors of shenanigans happening around the Ranch, but sneaking a whole-ass horse into one of the main buildings was a level up from what he'd expected.

"That was mighty bold of her," he said.

"Sure was," Arlo responded, a mix of disbelief, disapproval, and pride in his voice as he shook his head. "Wren got a very thorough spanking for that prank."

Maddie flushed, and Reid couldn't help but imagine taking the adorable Little girl over his knee to discipline when she'd been naughty. Although she seemed far too subdued to get in on hijinks like that—but maybe that wasn't how she always was.

He didn't know her very well, but he sensed a cloud of

sadness that seemed to overshadow her. Maybe some harmless antics would do her good. And if he got to spank her, so much the better.

* * *

SHE HAD to admit Peanut was pretty cute. He was small and not as intimidating as the bigger horses. He seemed to be pretty fond of Arlo too, nudging the man's hat and bumping his shoulder whenever Arlo had the nerve to stop petting him. She still wasn't in a hurry to get back on a horse, but visiting Peanut didn't seem awful.

"Is he that friendly with everyone or just you?" she asked, still tucked behind Reid. Yes, she'd peeked out from behind his arm to get a better view, but she wasn't ready to not have the broad wall of muscle between her and any horse.

"Oh, Peanut loves everyone, don't you, buddy?" Arlo said, rubbing the horse's neck.

"That was a good question, Maddie-girl. But it sounds like Peanut's pretty easygoing. Should I try petting him so you can see?"

She didn't want to let go of Reid, and her brain spun with trying to decide what she wanted less—to let go of her Daddy or to be closer to the horse.

"Um, okay," she allowed and then fisted her hands in the back of Reid's shirt. It was soft and worn, and the blues and browns and greys of the plaid were a good complement to his coloring. Not that he'd probably thought about that, but she sure was.

He tried valiantly not to chuckle at her but failed. Maddie didn't mind. Reid wasn't being cruel, and she had to admit it was ridiculous, using him as a human shield between her and what appeared to be a very sweet little horsey. Then again, Star had seemed very gentle—had been, actually—and she'd still ended up traumatized and bruised in the dirt. Hopefully there weren't any snakes in the stable. Darn sneaky snakes.

Reid took a few steps toward Peanut, and the horse blinked at him, sniffed the hand her Daddy held out, and then Reid was petting the animal. The horse's big jaw and, with another step, his long neck.

Peanut seemed to like the attention, and Maddie could understand why. She'd like Reid to pet her too.

Wait, what?

That thought had come out of nowhere. And would probably disappear just as quickly. She'd had sparks of interest in the past, and they'd always been snuffed out by the memory of Josh. But the vision of Reid stroking her hair and her cheek and possibly the rest of her body with those work-roughened hands didn't go away. Faded a bit, yes, but smoldered instead of being completely blown out. No, that wouldn't do at all.

To distract herself, she asked Arlo another question. "Is Peanut hungry?"

The corner of the stable hand's mouth turned up. "Do you mean is he gonna try to take a bite of you? Definitely not. He's already had his breakfast. You could give him a treat if you want, though. I've got some carrots and an apple."

She shook her head. Peanut might be small, but he still had big teeth—she wasn't ready to go near those chompers yet.

There was a noise at the far end of the stable, and Arlo's head snapped up.

"Sounds like I might be needed. You okay if I leave you

here with Peanut? He'll be a real good boy. You can brush him if you want; he likes that."

"We'll be fine," Reid assured him. "Thanks, Arlo."

The ranch hand ducked a nod and then jogged toward where the commotion had come from.

"Here, darlin', why don't you put your hand over mine and we can pet Peanut together?"

Maddie felt pretty ridiculous, but she let Reid peel her hand off his shirt and set it on the back of his. She had to move under his arm to reach the horsey, but that wasn't so bad. It was kind of nice to be pressed into Reid's side with his hand under hers.

He petted Peanut up by the horse's mane for a while, and Maddie found her curiosity getting the better of her.

"Can we trade?" she asked, looking up at Reid.

"Sure can."

It felt safe to be tucked under Reid's arm with his hand now covering hers. His protection and easy steadfastness lent her some bravery, and Maddie reached out, grazing fingertips over the long column of Peanut's neck. Reid applied a little pressure so her hand was flat against the horse's muscled flesh, and while she gasped, it actually felt nice to have more contact with the warm animal.

"That's it," Reid told her. "He's nice and soft, isn't he?"

"Mm-hmm."

Maddie stroked Peanut's neck a few more times, loving the way his shiny coat felt under her hand.

"You wanna know my favorite part of a horse?" Reid murmured, his breath warm against her ear.

"What?"

"Their noses. Softer than velvet."

"No way," she said, disbelieving.

"Yes way, darlin'. See for yourself. He's not gonna bite."

The promise of such fuzzy softness overcame her reluctance to have her fingers so close to Peanut's teeth. Plus, she'd been promised he wouldn't bite.

So she brushed her knuckles over the end of Peanut's snout and—Reid was right! The little horsey's nose was maybe the softest thing she'd ever touched, and she couldn't help but squirm and squeak with pleasure. Maybe horses were okay after all.

CHAPTER 10

They petted Peanut for a long time, and it was gratifying to watch Maddie get more comfortable with the foal. After a while of stroking him with their hands together, she reached up with her other hand and stroked his coat by herself. Once she seemed comfortable with petting him on her own, he grabbed some grooming tools.

It was so sweet how Maddie looked to him with her big blue eyes to make sure she was using the curry comb right. Almost gave him a toothache how lovingly and thoroughly she brushed Peanut's coat and combed out his mane and tail. How she giggled when he ate carrots out of her hand.

Made Reid feel like a big man to know he'd played a part in getting her from scared to even touch Peanut to loving on him like that. There wasn't anything quite like being a Little girl's Daddy, and even so, he'd never felt the way he did when he was encouraging Maddie, caring for her. Watching her succeed after she'd been so brave. It felt right in a way he'd never felt around a woman.

Eventually, the group came back from the trail ride, and Reid had an idea.

"Hey, darlin', can you stay here with Peanut while I ask Arlo something real quick?"

Anxiety flashed in her eyes, but then she steadied herself with a hand on Peanut's neck before stroking his mane.

"Yes, Sir. I can do that. We'll be just fine, won't we, Peanut?" She leaned in as if the horse were actually responding and then looked back to Reid. "He says yes."

Lord, that girl was cute.

"Alright, I'll be back in a jiff. You two behave while I'm gone."

Maddie nodded, and he ached to hear her say, *Yes, Daddy*. Hopefully soon.

"Hey, Arlo?"

"What's up?"

"You think Snickers might be up for another short, easy ride? Maybe with two people?"

The man considered for a moment and then nodded. "I think so. She wasn't too busy today. I'm guessing you're asking about taking Maddie out for a bit?"

Reid nodded his confirmation. He wasn't sure if he could talk Maddie into it, but he'd rather get permission first and have her say no than get her yes first and have her disappointed because there wasn't a horse available.

"She should be fine. She's a sturdy girl. Aren't you?" Arlo asked the horse, giving her neck a rub.

"Thanks, I'll owe you one."

"No trouble, that's what we're here for. Although if you wanted to look at my truck later, I wouldn't say no. It's been making this funny noise, and I exhausted my know-how."

"You got it," Reid told the stable hand with a clap on his shoulder.

A MEMORABLE LITTLE MEMORIAL DAY

He headed back to Maddie, who was still petting Peanut and talking to the foal. He was gonna be a real handsome horse someday, good-natured too.

"Hey, Maddie-girl. I just talked to Travis, and he said we could do something special."

"Peanut can have more carrots? He liked those."

For a girl who'd been terrified of horses a couple hours ago, she sure seemed to like Peanut just fine.

"No, Peanut's had his treats for the day. We don't want to give him a tummy ache, right?"

Maddie shook her head, eyes wide and earnest. There was something about being with the horses that made her seem more like a Little. Maybe because she trusted him to be more knowledgeable about them and more comfortable around them than she was. He liked how she looked at him when they were here. Wanted her to look at him like that all the time.

"What we can do is take Peanut's momma for a little ride."

The panic that lit her sweet face was enough to make him second-guess this plan, but no. She had to try again, and the sooner, the better. If she didn't get back in the saddle quickly, he didn't think she ever would, and she'd be missing out, big time.

He guessed she was far more likely to try it with him around than with someone who hadn't been labeled *Daddy*. Yep, he was going to put this under the heading of Duties of Maddie's Daddy, and he was gonna get her on a horse by the end of this week one way or another.

Reid walked closer, close enough to reach out and set a hand on her waist.

"Nothing to be afraid of. Snickers has been out on the trail all morning, so she's pretty tired. We're gonna double up, so I'll be right there with you, and she's the sweetest horse they've got. You know she's got to be a good one if Peanut is her son, right?"

Maddie looked skeptical as all get out.

"I don't think that's safe."

Reid didn't want to argue with her. First of all, it seemed unlikely he'd change the stubborn Little's mind. Also, he wanted her to trust him, not argue with him. There was only one thing to do: show, not tell.

"Why don't you at least come say hi to Snickers?"

Oh, this Little girl was going to be a challenge—the way she looked at him from under her brows was killer. Like she had *no* on the tip of her tongue. He wouldn't spank her for refusing, but he also didn't want to get to that point. So, before she could demur, he made her an offer he didn't think she'd be able to refuse.

"I don't think she's had her carrots yet today. Or maybe Arlo has an apple lying around?"

Fingers crossed Snickers hadn't already been spoiled with treats this morning, but with all these Littles running around, who knew what these horses got fed? He couldn't imagine how many pranks and shenanigans the horses had unwittingly been a part of either. Peanut ending up in the Littles' dorm was probably only the start of it.

Maddie perked up at the mention of giving Snickers treats.

"Come on," he said, beckoning to her with a hand. "Let's go ask Arlo."

* * *

A MEMORABLE LITTLE MEMORIAL DAY

Snickers had loved her apple, and Maddie had loved petting the mare. She did remind her a lot of Peanut, and her nose was almost as soft. Almost.

So, when Reid asked her if she wouldn't go on just a little ride, she said yes. Partly so she could see the approval light his face. That warmth in her belly was so nice; she'd missed it.

Reid swung up onto the mare first, looking like he'd been born to ride a horse, and then Arlo helped her settle in front of him. She was much less graceful than her Daddy had been, but neither Snickers nor Reid seemed to mind.

In fact, Reid gave her a kiss behind her ear that sent the most delicious shivers down her spine and said, "I'm so proud of you, little girl. Look at you, being so brave. We're going to have a nice, easy ride with Snickers. You just do what I say, and we'll go get a treat when we're done. Deal?"

"Deal."

Reid steered Snickers away from the stables toward a trail, and Maddie tried to relax and let her body move with the roll of the horse's stride. It was easier when she had Reid behind her, with his steady inhales and exhales to pin her breathing to.

"You can talk to her if you want," he told her. "She'll hear the tone of your voice even if she doesn't understand the words."

Maddie petted the side of Snickers's neck, and even though she felt kind of silly, she told the horsey, "You're a good girl, Snickers."

It was fun to watch the way her tall ears twitched backward, like she really was listening, and Maddie tugged on Reid's hand to make sure he saw.

"Yep, she's listening to you alright. Who doesn't like to be called a good girl?"

Maddie thought her chest might be on fire with the sudden bloom of warmth there. She wouldn't have been surprised if her face burst into flames. It was a good thing Reid couldn't see how much his words had affected her. She didn't want him to know either, so she spit out a question.

"Why do you know so much about horses, anyway? I thought you were a mechanic."

"I am. But I wasn't always a mechanic. I grew up on a ranch, riding horses, tending to 'em."

Riding on the trail was actually a lot of fun. Probably didn't hurt that she had Reid wrapped around her like a blanket. A really warm, muscly blanket who knew how to ride a horse.

She'd like to pretend she was completely unaffected by the way his pelvis rocked against her hips and how his thighs bracketed her own, but that would be a big, fat lie. She was going to have to get herself off as soon as she had a spare minute in the room she shared with Tamsyn.

Maybe this horse-riding thing wasn't so bad. Or so she thought until Reid asked, "You want to take the reins, Maddie-girl?"

"Oh no, definitely not."

She shook her head, probably whipping Reid in the face with her French-braided pigtails, and grabbed the pommel tighter with both hands.

"I think yes. Come on, I'll help."

Reid used his hand that wasn't holding the reins to gently prize her hands off the horn. Her heart pounded in her chest, and she felt as though the walls of her rib cage were closing in, but Reid's steady murmur in her ear and how his big hands sculpted around hers helped scatter the anxiety.

"There you go. That's a good girl," he told her as he arranged the reins in their entwined hands.

"In the Western style, you only hold the reins in one hand. That's how the cowboys used to do it. Know why?"

"Mmm..."

How was she supposed to know? She didn't know anything about cowboys! Except how good the one against her back felt and smelled. Mechanic schmechanic, Reid was definitely a cowboy.

There was something intoxicating about the scent of leather from Snickers's tack, the horse's warm earthy smell, the freshness of the wide-open air, and the green of the trees they were meandering through, plus the warmth of Reid. Was it possible for a person to smell like sunshine? Because she thought he might.

If she thought of Reid riding a horse on his own without her to slow him down, added a heroically cream-colored Stetson—this was a fantasy after all, no need to worry about dirt or anything else that might soil a hat—and some brown leather chaps over his jeans...

"Oh! Maybe because they had their lasso in the other hand?" she guessed and glowed when she could hear the smile in his voice when he responded.

"That's exactly it. You're real clever...for a city girl," he teased.

He squeezed his thighs around hers, and she could've melted into a puddle right on the horse.

"The horses on the Ranch have been trained in neck reining," he continued. "That means they change direction in response to light pressure on their necks. If you want the horse to go right..."

Reid moved their joined hands to the right, and

Snickers turned her head and started to walk a little toward the right.

"Now, what do you think you do if you want her to go left?"

Maddie did in fact want Snickers to go left because they were about to veer off the trail and that seemed like a very bad idea. So she shifted their hands to the left, which had the reins pressing lightly on the right side of Snickers's neck. Snickers took the cue and course corrected to get them back on the trail.

"That's right, you're a natural-born cowgirl. We'll have you barrel racing in no time."

"I don't think so."

She didn't know what barrel racing was, but it sounded fast and like a guaranteed way to fall off a horse again.

"Alright, we'll wait on the barrel racing. But maybe riding solo the next time we go out on the trail?"

There it was again, that *we*. Something else too. It wasn't just that she didn't want to ride alone because she was afraid of falling off again. She was also actively enjoying having Reid snugged up behind her.

"Mmm, maybe."

"Okay, Maddie-girl. I'll take *maybe*. For now."

CHAPTER 11

"You did a real good job today, darlin'. I'm proud of you for getting back on the horse again. Literally."

Reid's smile was intoxicating, as was his praise. It made her feel all warm and glowy inside.

He was walking her back to the main lodge after they'd taken another trail ride, building on her successful attempt yesterday. This afternoon they'd gone with other people, but Reid had arranged with Travis ahead of time for them to double up on Snickers again, and she'd been able to visit with Peanut and give him some treats beforehand.

So, while there'd been a brief burst of nerves, it had been pretty easy to climb up into the saddle in front of Reid again. Enjoy his warmth and strength at her back, his gentle encouragement in her ear.

Didn't hurt that she'd had a fun Tuesday morning of games and a picnic lunch with the other Littles, which Reid had dropped her off at and picked her up from. Maybe this Daddy-for-a-week business wasn't so bad.

"Thank you, Sir," she said, trying to ignore the butterflies in her tummy from the feel of Reid holding her hand.

He hadn't pushed her to call him *Daddy* yet, but she found more and more often that the title was on the tip of her tongue. She wanted to, but guilt had been holding her back.

"I promised Fitz we'd play some horseshoes this afternoon, so I thought I'd drop you off at the Littles' wing and you could go to a class. What do you think?"

Maddie pursed her lips. She thought it sounded really fun but also like maybe too much. Everything in the Littles' wing was dripping with red, white, and blue for Memorial Day. She respected and appreciated the patriotism, but it still made her heart heavy. She didn't know if she'd be able to glue some Popsicle sticks together or string beads when she was so sad.

Perhaps sensing her hesitation, Reid slowed to a stop. He took a step closer and slid a hand to cup her jaw while his thumb brushed her cheek.

"I don't think asking you is helpful. Just adds more fodder for your busy brain to chew on. So here's what's going to happen. You're going to go to art class and make a handprint eagle for me while I spend some time with Fitz. When I pick you up, we'll take a nap and then go to dinner with Tamsyn and Fitz like last night. Then we'll have some pool time before I put you to bed."

Maddie chewed on her lip because that all sounded really nice except for the craft project. Knowing how all in Rawhide went on everything, they'd probably be playing songs like "You're a Grand Old Flag" and "My Country 'Tis of Thee," and a bunch of the Littles would be singing or humming along while they labored over their artwork.

On the other hand, she didn't want to disappoint Reid or make him feel like he wasn't doing a good job as her Daddy. He was. Maybe too good.

"Yes, Sir," she agreed and was rewarded with another smile and a quick kiss to her forehead.

"That's my good girl. We'd better get a move on so you're not late. Don't want you getting a naughty slip."

Reid walked her to the classroom and passed her off to Nanny J. The whole day had been making her feel as though she was drifting into Little space, and being dropped off like this did nothing to change that. She'd like to give in and allow herself to bask in the glow of feeling small and cared for, and Reid was doing his best to let her. But every time she got too close to letting go, she reeled herself back in.

Tamsyn could make her go to a kinky ranch that specialized in DDlg and age play, but she couldn't force her into being Little. But really, who was Maddie hurting with her refusal? Didn't seem to be Tamsyn, who'd been doing a lot of the Middles activities and going to mixers and generally taking advantage of all the Ranch had to offer.

So maybe, maybe, she could loosen up a little. Give in to the part of her that wanted this relief so badly she could taste it. Almost as well as she could taste the grape juice and Goldfish crackers that had been set out for snacks in the corner of the classroom.

"I've gotta go now, little girl. Give Daddy a kiss," Reid instructed.

Maddie went up on tiptoes and pressed her lips to his cheek. His stubble prickled at her lips, and she loved the way he smelled when he was so close, loved how he patted her cheek when she sank back onto the soles of her feet.

"That's my sweet darlin'. Now have fun and be a good girl for Nanny J. I'll be back to get you in two hours."

* * *

When he picked Maddie up from the classroom, she seemed subdued. Not that she was one of the exuberant Littles who always seemed to be bouncing off the walls, but there was a difference between her quiet, dreamy distraction and whatever was going on now.

"Maddie was a very good girl," Nanny J told him as they walked over to the brightly colored craft table where she was sitting alone. "She followed all the directions, finished her project, and shared nicely with the other Littles. But I'm glad you're here. I think she might need some Daddy time."

Reid sure hoped that was true. Even though he'd had a good time beating the pants off his friend at horseshoes, he'd missed Maddie's presence. Had wished she was with him.

"Hey, darlin'," he said quietly as he squatted so he could be eye level with his Little girl. She did look out of sorts. Maybe it was just being overwhelmed by the boisterous Littles who were carousing around making a racket? He'd only been in here for a minute, and his ears were ringing. Or maybe her arm hurt? He'd get some ice on it after she woke up from resting. "You ready for nap time?"

She nodded wordlessly, and he noticed her eyes were sorta glossy. Not feverish but maybe a little teary. Maybe her arm was bothering her, although she didn't seem to be in pain.

"Can you show me your picture first, and then we'll get outta here, take a rest somewhere less like a zoo?"

Maddie nodded again and pulled her project closer to the edge of the table so he could see it. She'd done a real good job, and he told her so. But he also wondered how much fun she'd had doing it. Looked like maybe she'd focused too much on making it perfect and not enough on enjoying herself.

"Why don't you leave that overnight so it can dry, Maddie? You can pick it up tomorrow."

"Yes, Nanny J," she agreed.

The matronly woman smiled at her and then walked off to scold a couple Littles who'd gotten too rowdy on the other side of the room.

"C'mere, Maddie-girl," he said, beckoning to her. Her mouth formed a little frown, and he tsked at her. "I don't think you want to have that little bottom spanked for disobeying Daddy right before nap time, do you?"

She blinked at him, and he wondered if the threat had been too much, although spanking for disobedience had been part of the agreement they'd ironed out with Derek. But maybe she'd been thinking about something else because her shoulders dropped, and she said, "No, Daddy."

Hearing the words come out of her mouth made his heart skip. She'd called him *Daddy*. He wanted to demand she do it again, and again, and again, but he wouldn't. Maybe she'd switched from *Sir* since he'd taken the reins more firmly, and he didn't want to derail her. So plowing on, it was.

"Then come here," he instructed.

She might've been reluctant to do it, but once she was in motion, Maddie seemed drawn to him, holding out her arms to wrap around his neck. Once he'd stood, she rested her head on his shoulder and sighed.

Poor Little girl seemed plumb tuckered out. He'd have to revise his expectations for how much she could handle in a day. He could understand that. He could work all day at Mason's and have enough energy to still go to the shooting range, go for a hike, or help Fitz with some project, but a day spent around people—especially Littles who'd maybe had too much sugar because a few of them seemed to be going berserk—would have him beat.

He thanked Nanny J and carried Maddie back to his room, where he lay down with her on the bed, tugged her into his side. She fit perfectly against him.

"What's going on, little girl? You just tired from being around all those noisy Littles?"

"I don't want to talk about it, Daddy. Can that be okay for right now, please?"

He hated the idea of something bothering her that he didn't know about. A problem he couldn't solve, something broken he couldn't fix. It wasn't okay. He didn't like her withdrawing from him; he wanted her to seek him out.

For some Littles, insisting they share right now or get their bottoms blistered might work, but he didn't think Maddie was one of them. It would be far worse for her to clam up and resent him for punishing her than it would be to muster his patience and let her have her way for a bit. Still get to hear her call him *Daddy*.

"For now," he granted. "But you're still going to get Daddy cuddles while you take your nap. I'm not leaving you alone when you're feeling fragile."

"'Kay."

She snuggled into his side, her little body soft but chilled, and that wasn't going to do. Reid rolled her to right on top of him so he could easily feel her breathing. When Maddie struggled in his grasp and protested that she was too heavy, he smacked her backside lightly.

"You're like a baby bird—you're not too heavy. Also, I like you like this, so just settle down."

A MEMORABLE LITTLE MEMORIAL DAY

He tugged the blanket over them, which seemed to calm her, and it wasn't long before she was softly snoring deadweight while he held her close.

CHAPTER 12

When she woke up, she was still on top of Reid. And looking at the clock, she must've been that way for hours. Hopefully she hadn't drooled on him or snored or talked in her sleep.

She struggled to sit up, but of course he wouldn't let her. Instead he hugged her close to his chest and rolled the both of them upright so she was seated in his lap. That was nice but also horrifying.

The man she'd started calling *Daddy* was so close and so handsome and was giving her an indulgent smile.

"Evening, sleepyhead."

"Sorry I slept so long."

"Don't be sorry. If you were sleeping that soundly for that long, you clearly needed the rest. But it does mean Tamsyn and Fitz got hungry while you were napping and I told them it was okay to head to dinner without us. So it looks like it's just the two of us tonight," he said apologetically. "And since your arm needs to be iced, I thought we'd get some room service."

Oh dear. It was one thing to be in one of the restaurants

with Reid and his friend and Tamsyn. Fitz and Tamsyn bickered more like siblings and definitely didn't give off a couple vibe, so it was easier to pretend they were all just friends hanging out and everything was fine. Not weird or awkward at all.

But if she and Reid were alone in his room? That was far more intimate, and she didn't know if she could stomach it.

Before she could think too hard about it, though, he cupped his hands around her jaw and pressed a kiss to her forehead. That was really, really nice. Forehead kisses were the best. So tender and sweet, they seemingly had a hotline to her Little.

"Let's get you settled on the couch with some ice. It's looking more swollen. Maybe all that painting you did in art class aggravated it, or you slept with it at a funny angle."

She nodded, not knowing what to say and didn't argue as he swung his legs over the side of the bed and carried her over to the couch, where he set her down and tucked a blanket around her. She wasn't incapable, but she was still in the process of fully waking up, too muddled to grumble about being able to do it herself. Besides, her arm was hurting more than it had earlier in the day, so maybe he was right.

After he'd set her up with an ice pack, they looked through the menu together, then Reid rang room service and placed their order. He told her she could pick a movie to watch while they waited for their food—nothing above PG because Little girls didn't watch movies with bad language or too much violence in them.

Maddie could tell she was still pretty deep in Little space from her nap because having restrictions placed on what she could watch felt loving, like Reid was keeping her safe instead of being a controlling poopy head.

It wasn't too long before their food arrived. Once it had been delivered, Reid picked her up and walked over to the dining table with her on his hip.

She'd ordered grilled cheese and tomato soup, and Reid was having steak frites. Everything looked delicious. She also noticed that while Reid's plate and cutlery looked like any you'd find at a nice restaurant, hers did not. Her plate was pink and sparkly with a unicorn on it, and her grilled cheese had been cut into strips instead of halves. Her silverware and bowl matched the plate—pink and plastic with glitter all over, and they'd sent a small cup of fruit and a sippy cup filled with milk.

The Little inside her wanted to bounce in her seat with delight, but the rest of her felt vulnerable and raw. Most of the things she'd done at the Ranch so far were Little-ish, but there were adults who enjoyed lawn games and arts and crafts too. The presentation of this meal couldn't be shrugged off so easily.

Especially when Reid picked up a piece of fabric from the large tray and shook it out. It was a bib. Not a napkin like there was for him. A swath of white quilted cotton with a purple giraffe stitched on it. So cute it made her Little squee, but to grown-up Maddie, it might as well have been a scarlet letter.

"I don't think I can—"

"You can," Reid commanded. "And you will."

Maddie didn't want to be threatened with a spanking again so soon, so she gathered up her courage and capitulated. "Yes, Daddy."

He dropped a satisfied nod, and some of the tension in

her tummy unfurled. She'd been a good girl, and he was pleased with her. She really did like to be a good girl.

Her breath went shallow as he snapped the bib around her neck, and she swallowed hard. Reid straightened it just so and beamed at her.

"That's my pretty little Maddie-girl. Daddy's proud of you. Now be good and eat your dinner all up."

"Yes, Daddy."

Despite the warmth occupying her whole body—a concoction she suspected was equal parts embarrassment and arousal—she was hungry. It was easy to dip the grilled cheese sticks into the tomato soup and eat it that way, but she was going to run out of grilled cheese way sooner than she was going to run out of soup. And it was so good—she didn't want it to go to waste.

First she reached for the spoon with her right hand but was quickly reminded that wasn't a good idea with her arm still kind of swollen and definitely still sore even though her Daddy had just made her ice it. So she switched to her left, and that was a different problem entirely.

The grilled cheese had been pretty easy to handle, but the spoon—even though it was made for Littles—was much more challenging to maneuver. She managed to get some of the soup to her mouth, but she spilled a few drops on the table that Reid quickly mopped up with a napkin.

"Silly Maddie," he scolded gently. "Here, let Daddy feed you so you don't make a mess."

In truth, she could imagine snuggling into his arms while he gave her a bottle, but that was in the privacy of her own mind, and she was not going to share. Besides, she already had her hands full with a very real, very handsome Reid extending his hand and waiting expectantly for her to give over the spoon.

"Give it here now, little girl. Don't make me ask you again."

Reluctantly, she surrendered the spoon, her tummy flipping as she did. It wasn't a bad feeling exactly, but it made its way to her heart, making it thump against her rib cage.

Reid scooped up some of the soup and held it aloft a few inches in front of her.

"Open up, darlin'," he commanded.

As so often happened when she was with him, Maddie's body obeyed without her brain's buy-in, and she parted her lips enough for him to slip the spoon into her mouth and then sipped the creamy tomato blend, letting it slide down her throat.

How did soup taste better when she ate it off a spoon held by her Daddy's hand? But it did. Oh yes, it did. *Everything* felt better somehow. As Reid fed her spoonful after spoonful, her muscles relaxed, and everything seemed to fuzz into soft focus. Everything except Reid. Daddy. Her Daddy. He was just as sharp and clear as ever. Near-black hair and ice-blue eyes, the stubble that only served to emphasize his square jaw, and the dimple that would appear only when he smiled really big.

She didn't argue at all when he used the last few grilled cheese sticks to mop up the remainder of the soup and fed those to her, even though she could do that part herself. No, she liked how he waited for her to chew and swallow and then offered her the next bite. Even how he dabbed at her mouth with a napkin.

"You full, little girl?"

"Yes, Daddy."

"Feeling pretty Little?"

"Mm-hmm, Daddy."

His indulgent smile made her want to climb into his lap,

and since being fed had busted up some of her inhibitions, she did. Just walked over and stood in front of him until his eyes lit with understanding and he pushed his chair out, drew his knees together, and patted his thigh.

"That's right, sweet girl, come sit with Daddy."

Maybe it was her full tummy or possibly that she was still recovering from her horse mishap, but it wasn't so long before her head was lolling against Reid's shoulder. He cradled her there and then started to sing. So quiet she had to listen really hard to parse out the words, but it was a nice song about a baby horse and a momma horse. Maddie fell asleep to visions of horses galloping through fields, safe in her Daddy's lap.

* * *

Was it possible for a man's dick to bruise? He might find out, because having Maddie nestled snug against him after she'd let him feed her most of her dinner was making him damn hard.

The last thing he wanted to do was disturb her, but as much as he might like to hold her in his lap all night, he couldn't. He didn't think she'd appreciate waking up in his bed in the morning either. He'd been surprised she didn't resist taking a nap in his room. But even if he'd thought she would be okay having a sleepover with Daddy, he didn't have any of her things here.

Quietly and smoothly as he could, Reid picked up his Little girl and headed down the hall to Maddie and Tamsyn's suite. Used the key card Derek had given him as Maddie's Daddy to let himself and his out-like-a-light Little into her room. Once inside, he brought her over to the bed and laid her down.

She was still in her clothes, and he couldn't let her sleep like that. Not in her skirt with the button in the front that would dig into her soft tummy and not in that bra. He had sisters and had listened to them complain many times about how uncomfortable those damn things were.

If Maddie were his, there would be no bras allowed unless they were going someplace where she had to be proper. Mostly he wanted her in onesies and jumpers and drop-seat pajamas. Clothes that would keep a Little girl comfy.

First things first. Ignoring his throbbing dick, he unbuttoned and unzipped her skirt, shimmied the denim and cotton down her legs and then draped the skirt over a nearby chair. Her panties were the cutest thing he'd ever seen—they looked like a slice of watermelon with the green and white of the rind at her waist and then a pretty pink dotted with black seeds covering her mound and her sweet pussy.

Good thing his jeans were made for withstanding some hard labor because otherwise his erection would've busted out the fly by now. Untying the knot of her shirttails at her waist and then unbuttoning the crisp white cotton shirt didn't help any, especially when he saw her matching bra. Watermelon slices cupped her small breasts, and he bet suckling on her would be just as sweet as taking a bite of the fruit. Christ, he needed a cold shower.

She stirred when he slid his hands underneath her to undo the clasp, looking bleary-eyed and muddled in his direction. "Daddy?"

"Shh, Maddie-girl. Daddy's just getting you ready for bed. You need your comfy pj's on."

"Uh-huh," she agreed. "Where's Cleopatra?"

Right, her beloved stuffie. Luckily the manatee was close by, and he gave her the well-loved toy to hold on to.

"You snuggle with Cleo while Daddy gets you some jammies. I'll be right back."

He should've thought to get her pajamas before he stripped her, but he was lucky there was enough blood circulating in his brain that he remembered how to breathe, never mind think. Luckily, he found a matching camisole and shorts set made of soft, stretchy material in the first drawer he looked in and brought the sunshine-yellow outfit over to the bed where Maddie hadn't moved.

Except she had. Just enough to tuck her thumb into her mouth. She was so goddamn cute he was going to expire. But first he'd get her into her pajamas and tucked in.

Once Maddie was settled, thumb back in her mouth and holding Cleopatra against her chest, he sat on the couch. It was tempting to go into the girls' bathroom and relieve himself of this ache either through rubbing one out or jumping into a freezing cold shower, but he was supposed to be a Daddy. A man who had enough restraint that he could handle himself and still have plenty of discipline left over for a Little girl. Being a creepy and incorrigible jerk-off did not scream self-control.

It wasn't easy to fight off all the images of being with Maddie that were flooding his brain. His imagination conjured pictures of them playing board games together, maybe coloring if she liked to do that when she was Little. He really tried to steer clear of thinking sexy thoughts about her.

What was the point of daydreaming about those things anyway? They were only here for a week. Maddie didn't seem inclined to open up too quick, and he wasn't in the business of breaking Littles, so he might not get much further with her along any dimension.

Even if she was open as the prairie wildflowers at this time of year, he wasn't the kind of man to take a girl like that on. One who deserved someone who would make promises and keep them. A Little girl who needed a forever Daddy. Never had been and never would be, and he'd do well to remember that instead of pining over the Sleeping Beauty he could never have. Not the way she'd need having.

It was a few hours of lounging on the couch messing around on his phone before Tamsyn returned from wherever she'd been that evening. He probably could've—maybe should've—left, just written Maddie a note to call if she needed anything, but he couldn't bring himself to do it. Instead he got to endure Maddie's friend's knowing smirk as he waved a silent goodbye and headed back to his own bunk.

CHAPTER 13

A couple days later, Tamsyn had Maddie by the hand of her good arm and was trying to haul her off the couch.

"Come on, Maddie, please? How can you not want to go to a water balloon fight? It's going to be so much fun!"

Being hit with projectiles that would explode cold water on her upon contact did not sound like "so much fun" to her. Or any fun at all. It sounded ouchie and wet and cold. Not her idea of a good time on a Thursday afternoon.

"I think I'll just stay here and watch some TV. I'm kind of tired, and besides, I won't be able to throw properly with my arm like this."

In truth her arm was feeling about 75 percent better. When her Daddy had brought her by the infirmary today so Nurse Mac could check her over, the older woman had seemed very pleased with her progress.

"Your Daddy must be doing a very good job of making sure you followed instructions about icing. That bruising will stick around for a bit, but you'll be good as new."

She didn't feel good as new. Not her arm and definitely not her brain. She'd had fun over the past couple days doing some Littles' activities, hanging out with Tamsyn, and, of course, spending time with Reid. He picked her up every morning, walked her between activities, lay down with her while she napped, and tucked her into bed with Cleopatra at night.

They would often have meals together, just the two of them or with Fitz and Tamsyn. Sometimes he took her to the pool or to one of the playgrounds, and he insisted she get on a horse every day. He said she could do whatever she wanted as long as it involved riding, but what she wanted was to double up on Snickers and have a leisurely trail ride. She wondered sometimes if her cowboy Daddy didn't get impatient with such a boring outing, but he never seemed to mind.

He'd dropped her off at her room so she could spend some time with Tamsyn before dinner, and she'd fully intended to, but... It was hard to have fun and be chipper when you had a guilty conscience.

Tamsyn pouted but let go of her arm.

"Are you sure it's really your arm that's bothering you?" her bestie asked pointedly.

They both knew it wasn't, and Maddie felt her cheeks get warm from telling the little lie. If Reid knew, she'd get her bottom spanked, which she'd managed to avoid so far. But Tamsyn wouldn't rat her out. Probably.

"I just can't today," Maddie said, shaking her head. "I swear I'm doing my best but..."

She shrugged helplessly. If she knew how to wipe away her shame and despondency, she'd do it. Well, that was a lie. But it didn't matter, now did it? Because there was no cure, there was no medicine, there was no treatment for this kind of heartbreak.

"Okay," her friend granted with a sigh that said she'd let

her get away with not joining in the reindeer games but wasn't happy about it. "But you're coming to dinner. It's a mac and cheese bar at dinner tonight, and I know you don't want to miss that."

She didn't. And Reid wouldn't let her anyway.

"I will see you for dinner. Pinky swear."

* * *

REID KNOCKED on the door to Tamsyn and Maddie's suite and tried to hide his disappointment when Tamsyn opened the door. He liked Maddie's friend. A lot, actually. Probably because she and Fitz were a lot alike. Sarcastic assholes who were too smart for their own good.

Despite his dubious taste in friends, he had excellent taste in Little girls. He was really looking forward to seeing Maddie tonight. Dinner for the Bigs was surf and turf, and the Littles were having a mac and cheese bar. He'd worn his nicest shirt for the occasion, and he'd texted Maddie earlier to tell her to wear a pretty dress. It was nice to spend time with her no matter what she wore, but he couldn't wait to see his little darlin' all dolled up.

He and Fitz had gone to a whip class taught by Derek himself, and while Reid wasn't sure a whip would ever be his implement of choice—too far away from the woman he was playing with—it was always a good time to listen while people who were passionate and knowledgeable talked about something they loved.

It had also maybe stoked the sadistic fire inside him to see Derek whip his perky wife. Made him want to take Maddie over his knee and make her squirm and squawk and cry.

She'd consented to being spanked for punishment but

not for pleasure, and so far she hadn't stepped a toe out of line. Which, of course, he was glad for—her obedience and model behavior were a treasure—but his hand still itched.

Fitz had told him to go seek someone else out at one of the play parties or in a workshop so he could get his fix, but the idea hadn't appealed. He didn't want to spank *someone*; he wanted to spank Maddie. Wanted to soak in her submission, wanted to relish her cries of pain like nursing a really good bourbon, wanted to kiss away her tears and tell her how proud and grateful Daddy was.

Tamsyn frowned back, and despite his own reaction to her, he was a little insulted. Maddie's bestie had seemed like the biggest fan of their relationship. Maybe more excited about it than Maddie herself, but that was a bone he'd gnaw on another day.

"Evening, Tamsyn. Maddie here?"

The blonde's frown deepened as she shook her head. "No, I thought she was with you."

Worry started to stew in his gut. Maddie and Tamsyn had more leeway than the Littles who stayed in the dorms, but Derek had made it clear Maddie wasn't to wander about by herself. She was free to be escorted by her roommate or her Daddy, but she should be with one of them unless she was in her room or in the Littles' wing.

"No. I haven't seen her since I dropped her off here with you this afternoon."

This wasn't good.

"Try calling her," Fitz suggested.

"Mind if we come in?" Reid asked Tamsyn before stalking through the open door.

"Yeah, of course."

The three of them headed for the seating area, but no

one sat. Tamsyn and Reid both had their phones out, and the blonde made eye contact with him.

"You call and I'll text?"

He nodded, the disquiet wending its way from his stomach and up to his chest, making it hard to draw full breaths.

"I'll call Nanny J," Fitz volunteered. "See if Maddie didn't end up in the Littles' wing somehow."

Reid hoped so. Because when he'd wished to spank Maddie, he certainly hadn't had in mind that it'd be a punishment for pulling a disappearing act.

CHAPTER 14

They'd been searching for a couple hours now, and it was dark. He was losing his goddamn mind. Maddie couldn't have just...disappeared into thin air, but hell if he knew where she could be.

After getting confirmation from Nanny J that Maddie was not in the Littles' wing, Reid had called Derek to tell him Maddie was missing. God love him, Reid didn't think the man could've been any more concerned if it had been Sadie who couldn't be located, but he was also keeping a cool head. Of course, Lawson, the head of security, was also on the case.

A bare-bones crew had been left to staff dinner, the front desk, and the Littles' wing, but otherwise every Ranch employee was out on the property looking for Maddie. They'd checked everywhere, called and texted her incessantly.

He couldn't help but think the worst, and it would be all his fault if something had happened to her. He was her Daddy, and he was supposed to look after her. He was supposed to be there for her and earn her trust so she could tell him anything. Yeah, it had only been a few days, but she'd been warming to him more and more, and he'd thought they'd made real good progress. Apparently not good enough.

He and Tamsyn were back in the girls' suite after being out searching, but he couldn't sit around and do nothing. Anything would be better than feeling useless and bungling.

"I'm gonna go check her favorite places again," he told Tamsyn. "You should stay here and wait for her in case she comes wandering in with no idea the whole place has been in an uproar."

Maddie's friend gave him a sad smile. "God, I hope so."

"Me too. I'll call you with any updates."

"Same," Tamsyn promised.

He stopped first at the Jacuzzi area outside their suite and then the pool. Maddie was a real good swimmer and loved being in the water. He'd told her she swam like a fish, and she'd frowned then said, *No, Daddy. Not a fish. A mermaid.*

She was so adorable it killed him. He'd never forgive himself if something had happened to her.

No sign of her in the center of the resort or at the outdoor playground. So he headed down toward the stables. A few days ago, he would've laughed if someone had suggested his Maddie-girl would ever go near horses voluntarily. She was still a little wary around most of them, but she'd become pretty attached to Peanut and Snickers. Wasn't a sillier place to look than anywhere else.

The stables were quiet when he got there since Jagger and Travis and Arlo and the other hands on duty had looked through the place already, including the tack room and the hayloft. Even if she wasn't here, maybe it would do him some good to be around horses. He'd done that a lot as a kid. If he'd had a real rough day at school or fought with his folks, saddling up a horse for a ride or just petting or grooming one had been able to settle him a bit.

He checked everywhere—the tack room, bathrooms, hayloft—and then proceeded down the line of stalls, opening and entering every single one. Not that he could imagine Maddie actively trying to hide from him or anyone else, but he'd run out of other options. At least any he could live with.

Stomach in knots and heart heavy, he went into Snickers's stall and petted the friendly mare for a few minutes. Didn't make him feel any better at all, but it was nice to express his worst fears out loud to the big animal with the kind eyes.

He closed and latched Snickers's gate then went next door to Peanut's stall. At first he didn't see the foal, but when he let himself in, he realized it was because the little horse was lying down in the front corner.

And just barely visible behind him was something bright pink.

* * *

MADDIE HAD BEEN HAVING the weirdest but most wonderful dream. She was a mermaid princess, and Peanut was a seahorse, and he was big enough for her to ride, not like in real life. They'd been riding—swimming?—through kelp forests and coral reefs, and she'd just stumbled upon a very handsome merman who looked suspiciously like Reid—

It was very annoying that her mom was trying to get her up for school. Or maybe it was Tamsyn telling her it was time for work? But then why did everything smell like hay and horse and—

Oh no.

Her eyes flew open, and she roughly pulled the earbuds from her ears.

Reid was standing over her, and then he was hefting her into his arms for a giant bear hug and squeezing her so tight she couldn't breathe.

"Daddy? Wha—"

"You scared us all to death, Maddie-girl. Thank God you're okay. Jesus, little girl..."

Just when she thought she might have to safeword, Reid set her down and looked her up and down, chafing her arms with his big hands.

"You okay? You're not hurt?"

"I'm fine, Daddy. Promise."

The cobwebs in her brain were still clearing—she'd apparently been very deeply asleep—and confusion was creeping in to take its place.

Reid put a hand over his heart and took a deep breath. "I have some calls to make, and then you and I are going to have a very long talk."

That...did not sound good. It sounded like his hand was going to have a very long talk with her butt, and she didn't know why.

He guided her out of Peanut's stall and stood just outside, wrapped an arm around her to hold her close, and then ordered, "Give Daddy a hug, darlin'. And don't let go until I say."

"Yes, Daddy," she murmured, wrapping her arms around his lean waist and pressing her head into his chest.

Then he was talking into his phone.

"Tamsyn, I found her. At the stables. She's alright. I'll call Derek and Fitz. Can you call Lawson and Nanny J?

She stood there holding on tight to Reid while he made a few other calls, all sounding a lot like the one he'd made to Tamsyn. Had everyone been looking for her? And why? She hadn't been gone for that long, had she? But looking around the stable, the light wasn't streaming in from outside, it was coming from lamps overhead. And Reid's conversations made it sound like everyone thought she'd been missing...

Finally, Reid hung up from his last call and squeezed her hard with both arms. It had always been nice that he was so strong, but now that he was wrapped around her like a boa constrictor, she thought maybe he was too strong.

Before she could ask any of her many, many questions, he was hefting her into his arms and carrying her like a baby monkey. She wrapped her legs around his waist and considered asking if she could say good night to Peanut but thought better of it. Her Daddy did not seem in the mood.

When they got to the room he shared with Fitz, he sat with her on the couch and insisted she have some water and a snack. Once she was done, he made her stand in front of the foot of his bed where he then sat.

Having him not touching her and the very stern look on his face made her feel very naughty, and she hated the sinking feeling in her stomach. She hadn't meant to be bad; she'd just needed some space.

"You're gonna tell me what happened, Maddie-girl. Everything starting from when I dropped you off at your room."

She swallowed hard and wrapped her fingers around the cuffs of her hoodie.

"I hung out with Tamsyn for a while, and then she went

to the water balloon fight. I didn't want to go. I thought I'd just watch some TV, but there was nothing on, and I didn't feel like reading my book, so I decided to go for a walk."

"You're not supposed to leave your room or be outside the Littles' wing without a Big. You know that."

"I do, but Tamsyn was gone, and you were busy with Fitz and I…"

Ugh, her Daddy crossing his arms over his broad chest made her feel like she was going to puke.

"You what? Decided to ignore the rules when they were inconvenient?"

Yep, the way her stomach was pitching made her wish Reid hadn't insisted she eat something. But in addition to the sick, in-trouble feeling, there was some anger too.

Part of her wanted to argue. She hadn't asked to come to this Ranch in the first place! Yes, she'd agreed to follow the rules, but they were silly rules. She was a grown-up, darn it. She'd been paying her own bills and taking care of herself—mostly—for five whole years now, and if she had to do all the stuff she hated, then she should at least be able to take a walk without a chaperone. So what if she'd just wanted to be alone? Take a walk to clear her head? Why should that be against the rules? It made her want to scream and stomp her foot.

But another part of her realized she was being defensive because Reid was right. She'd made a promise, and she'd broken it. That was black-and-white, and arguing was not going to get her anywhere.

"Yes, Daddy," she admitted, feeling the tears gather.

"Okay," Reid said with a nod. "Now tell me the rest."

"I walked down to the stables and decided to say hi to Peanut. I promise I didn't give him any treats."

She'd definitely thought about it, but she hadn't wanted to give him a tummy ache.

"That's good, darlin'. I know you wouldn't want to make him sick."

She took a deep breath and continued, "It was nice to just be in there with him. I petted him for a long time, and then I got kind of sleepy. So I thought I would sit down and rest for a few minutes before I walked back up to the main building. It's pretty far."

Reid looked unimpressed with her logic but didn't say anything. Best to just spill the rest of the story, rip the Band-Aid off.

"I put my earbuds in and put on one of the calming tracks from this app I like and sat in the corner of Peanut's stall. I guess I must've fallen asleep because the next thing I remember is you waking me up."

He didn't need to know about the mermaid dream, no way. Especially since that was the first time she'd dreamed about someone other than Josh.

CHAPTER 15

"Do you have anything else you want to say?"

"I'm sorry, Daddy."

She did look real sorry, standing there in her denim jumper, bright pink hoodie, and her striped knee socks. Hell, she still had some straw in her hair even though he'd tried to pick it all out while he'd been making his calls.

"That's good, but sorry is not going to cut it, young lady. You intentionally broke the rules, and you didn't tell anyone where you were. Do you know how worried I was about you?"

"No."

Well, she was going to learn real soon. He'd had a few flashes of anger once he'd found her safe, but they'd been brief in comparison to the downpour of relief that had washed over him, like lightning during a prairie storm.

The anger had all left him now, otherwise he wouldn't dare touch her. Not to punish her anyway. Wouldn't be fair to her because a person who was angry was a person not in control. The aim of disciplining Maddie wasn't to scare her, not at all, but to drive the point home about following rules —rules that were there for good reason. And also to have her pay her penance so she wouldn't be haunted by her disobedience the rest of her life.

"I was terrified when we figured out you were missing, and that didn't let up until I found you hours later. I thought something real bad had happened to you, like you'd drowned in the lake or gotten lost in the sapphire mines, maybe got bit by a rattlesnake. My mind went wild."

Reid didn't think of himself as a particularly creative man, more of a practical nuts-and-bolts sort, but his imagination sure had gone into overdrive about all the terrible things that could've happened to his Little girl.

"Everyone was in a panic. Did you think about how I would feel if I came looking for you and couldn't find you? What about Tamsyn? What about all the other people at this Ranch who are responsible for your safety, everyone here who's been your friend? Master Derek and Sadie? Jagger? Nanny J? Travis and Wren? Did you think about anyone but yourself when you went on your little walk?"

"No, Daddy." She sniffed. "I'm sorry. I'm so sorry. I'll never wander off again, I promise."

"No, you will not. Now come here. You're going over my lap, and you're not getting up until you've learned your lesson."

She wanted to argue, he could see it in her eyes. But there was something else there too. He might even call it need.

"Come here, Maddie-girl. Daddy's not going to ask again," he told her and held out his hand.

That was what she'd needed, for him to reach out just a little more. Maddie slipped her soft, small hand into his, and something protective and possessive surged through him as he closed his fingers around hers and pulled her closer.

Reid sat her on his knee, loving the way her feet dangled a few inches off the floor. He would let her go if she safed out, but until she did, he was in charge here, and she was going to understand that. Using a rough grip on her hip, he tugged her closer until her shoulder was flush against his chest and then took hold of her jaw, squeezing until her lips parted.

"Wandering off like that and not telling anyone where you'd gone was very naughty," he told her. "Little girls can get lost real easy. Or you could've gotten hurt, and we wouldn't know where to look for you. You had this whole Ranch in a tizzy searching for you. Is that what you wanted? Some attention?"

She tried to shake her head but couldn't get far because of how he was holding her. And her "no, Daddy" came out kind of muffled.

"Because you know if you need attention, all you've got to do is find me."

* * *

WHEN WAS the last time someone had made her a promise like that? Yes, she knew she could call Tamsyn anytime and her friend would be there for her, and it didn't have to be for an emergency. But she would feel far too ridiculous to seek her friend out just because she wanted attention.

The last time someone had told her he would be there for whatever she needed... Well. Her brain went all staticky and sadness swamped her. Reid could promise that now, but he'd leave her too. At least she knew when that was coming; their relationship had a very firm expiration date.

"I'm not angry with you. No one is angry with you. We're all relieved you're safe. I understand that falling asleep was an accident and that you didn't hear the people searching the stable the first time because you had your earbuds in and your music on. But you broke the rules, and breaking the rules means you get punished."

Her stomach clenched. She wasn't afraid of Reid. He would never really hurt her. And she knew Master Derek and Jagger and Travis and Arlo and everyone else on the Ranch would never let anyone near a Little if they thought that person might harm them. But she was still nervous.

It had been a long time since she was punished, but she doubted she would like it any more now than she had then. But that was the point, wasn't it? Punishments weren't supposed to be fun.

And maybe it was weird, but part of her wanted it. Wanted Reid to spank her until it hurt so she could feel bad. Because when Josh had punished her when she'd messed up, she'd felt the guilt and the yuckiness in her tummy clear away like clouds burned away by the sun. That forgiveness and absolution had felt really good. Even if her mind had tried to trick her into feeling bad about it again, Josh was there to remind her she'd done her penance and there was no need to keep playing that tape over in her head.

Reid was gentle as he placed her across his lap and rubbed her low back. "That's it. Settle down, Maddie-girl. No need to be in a tizzy."

Easy for him to say. He wasn't the one who was about to get spanked. But she would keep that to herself because no doubt sass would only add some swats to her punishment, and she didn't need a sorer bottom than absolutely necessary.

"Now I'm going to pull your dress up and your panties down because this kind of behavior definitely warrants a bare-bottom spanking. You make sure you use your safeword if you need to. You remember what safewords are not for?"

"I shouldn't use my safeword just because getting spanked is ouchie."

"That's right, good girl. I can guarantee it's going to be ouchie. And you remember what they're for too?"

"If I get scared or if it hurts in a way it's not supposed to or if it's really too much."

"I'm gonna add if you feel really uncomfortable for this punishment. You and I don't know each other real well, and I know baring your butt to a near stranger is tough. It's supposed to be embarrassing, alright? But I don't want you to feel unsafe."

"Yes, Daddy."

Maddie found it difficult to believe she could ever feel unsafe with Reid. Yes, he was about to swat her butt until it was stinging and red, but that didn't make her afraid. He was always so gentle with her, even when he was pushing her, even when she'd wandered off and he'd lost his mind with worry.

She did feel a creep of humiliation as he turned her skirt over her back and tugged her panties down to midthigh. No one had seen her like this for years, and certainly not someone who was basically a stranger. Mortified, yes; afraid, no.

The first touch of Reid's hand was as he smoothed his calloused palm over the curve of her backside, and it made her sigh. She couldn't forget she was about to be punished, but it still felt good to have him rubbing her skin. Maybe when he was done, he would put some cream on her bottom before he sent her on her way? She could hope.

"Alright, darlin'. We're gonna get started now. If you start flailing around, I'm gonna hold you down so neither of us gets hurt, but your safeword always works. Cross my heart."

The first smack landed on her right cheek, and she whimpered. Yeah, that smarted and stung, and she knew it would only get worse. She didn't think Reid would go too hard on her, but she also knew him well enough to know he wouldn't take it easy on her either.

It was annoying—and painful—in some ways, but it also made her feel strong and respected. Reid didn't think she was weak. He would push her out of her comfort zone, but he'd always held her hand while he did. After a few minutes during which the swats got harder and harder and he covered from just below her tailbone all the way down to the tops of her thighs, there was a spank so hard that Maddie couldn't help but fling her hands backward to protect herself.

Reid didn't seem angry that she'd moved after he'd told her to be still, but he did gather her hands up to cross her wrists behind her and press them into the small of her back, and he shifted so her legs were now trapped between his powerful thighs.

"Does your arm hurt like this?"

"No, Daddy."

"Good. That's the kind of bad hurt I mean. I can't have you wriggling around like a squirmy little worm. Your punishment should hurt only how I mean for it to. I'm gonna hold you down so neither one of us gets injured.

You're not bad for needing help staying still. I knew this was going to happen. You understand?"

"Yes, Daddy," she said, grateful that he'd made the distinction and assured her that she wasn't naughty for not being able to stay still. Who would be able to stay still with their bottom getting whaled on like this?

CHAPTER 16

With Reid raining hard-as-heck spanks down over her whole backside, Maddie didn't last long before she was crying, really hard. *So* hard. Her butt felt like it was on fire, so hot she wouldn't be surprised if she saw flames when she looked over her shoulder or if she smelled smoke. It hurt so much it stole her breath.

Just when she thought she'd have to choke out her safeword because she just could not handle this anymore, her Daddy stopped. Released her hands and legs and cuddled her on his lap.

It was a little funny that she wanted nothing more than to cling to him, have him hold her and tell her kind things after he'd been the one to tan her hide, but...that's what she wanted. His comfort, his approval. To know she was back in his good graces and that she was forgiven.

"That's it, little girl. You're okay. Your spanking's over now, and you did a real good job. I'm so proud of you for not arguing with me. I know that can be hard."

Her Daddy held her and rocked her on his lap until she'd mostly stopped the waterworks. When she could bring herself to look up at him, there was no anger or disappointment in his eyes.

"There's my sweet darlin'," he said, wiping away the tears that hadn't soaked into his shirt. "Daddy's good girl."

Oh good, she was still his good girl. Her heart would've broken if he never called her *Maddie-girl* again or *darlin'* in that soft Western twang.

"Your spanking's all done, but there's one more part of your punishment left."

There was *more*? Now she wanted to protest. Hadn't Reid taken his pound of flesh? Wasn't she sorry and sore enough already? Was he going to give her corner time or maybe make her write lines? She hated both those things, but she would do them if that's what her Daddy thought was fair.

"What is it, Daddy?"

"We're gonna go to Master Derek's office, and you're going to apologize to him and Jagger and Lawson."

Oh no. That would be so awful. She liked Master Derek even if he was a little scary, and Jagger had been so kind to her. She didn't know the head of security well, but he was sort of like a British version of her Daddy, so she sort of liked him by default. She knew those men must know about her disobedience, and had probably been among the people out looking for her. It was going to be bad enough to see them around the Ranch until she left...

"What's going on in that head of yours, Maddie-girl?"

"I was going to ask if I could just write them notes"—which she hadn't actually expected Reid to agree to—"but I think I figured out why you want me to say sorry in person."

"And why's that?"

"I just started worrying about seeing them and everybody else around the Ranch for the rest of the week. Thinking they must hate me and wanting to hide so I wouldn't feel so awful. But if they accept my apology and I can see it, I think I'll feel better."

She didn't expect Reid to smile at her, but he did.

"That's exactly right, darlin'. You're awful clever for a city girl."

Even though she was still sniffly, a giggle bubbled up from her chest at his joke. Yes, Reid was a very good Daddy. Thorough and thoughtful and caring. She was going to miss him after they headed their separate ways on Tuesday.

"Let's get you straightened up so we can get that taken care of."

A few minutes later, she shuffled into Master Derek's office feeling awful. She was certain her face was red and splotchy from being so embarrassed and from all her crying. Her backside was still on fire, and the idea of having to see these men who were disappointed in her made her stomach riot. But holding hands with her Daddy, she did it.

Master Derek and Jagger and Lawson were all standing behind Master Derek's big desk. The only thing she was grateful for was that Master Derek wasn't going to use that scary-looking paddle on his wall on her already-battered bottom.

Reid stood her in front of the desk and then said, "Now turn around, pull your panties down, and bend over, darlin'. You're going to show them your blistered bottom while you say you're sorry."

Oh, this was too terrible to bear.

"Daddy, I can't," she whispered, clutching her hands in her skirt. The idea of the men seeing her...her butt and that she'd been spanked...hard... Was it possible to die of humiliation? Could she maybe skip the humiliation part and just die?

"Yes, you can, Maddie-girl. I know you can because you're very brave and very strong. I also know you're really, truly sorry for making everyone worry about you."

"I am," she assured him, hoping Reid would understand the tremble in her voice not as fear but as an indication of how truly apologetic she was.

"I know you are, darlin'. All I'm asking you to do is show Master Derek and Jagger and Lawson how sorry you are. And when you're done, it's all over. All is forgiven, the slate is wiped clean, and you don't have to think about it ever again."

She wanted that, so badly. So, as sick as it made her, Maddie gathered up every ounce of courage she had. She turned around, pulled her dress up to her waist, slid her underwear down to just below her butt cheeks, and reached for her toes.

* * *

It was so hard to listen to his Little girl sobbing and choking out her apologies. She was hurting so bad, and her pain stabbed him right in the heart. He knew he was doing the right thing because this was certainly a lesson she'd never forget, but would she resent him afterward? It was more important that she was safe than that she was his, but goddamn if he didn't want both.

He'd never touch her again if she didn't want him to, but he'd feel the loss of her down to the marrow of his bones.

Finally, Maddie managed to say her last sorry in between her halting sobs. When she was done, she fell to her knees and buried her face in her arms. Every particle of him ached to go to her, but Derek held up a finger before rounding the desk and sinking to his knees next to the sobbing Little girl, resting a hand on her lower back.

"I accept your apology, Maddie. And so do Lawson and Jagger. We'll make sure everyone else knows how sorry you are too. Now, why don't you sit up so I can see that pretty face of yours?"

Ribs still heaving and tears still streaming down her cheeks, Maddie did as she was told, sitting back on her heels, which must smart like hell. He'd given her quite a hiding.

"There you are," Derek said and took a handkerchief out of his pocket to dab at her cheeks. "Now go along with your Daddy. He's going to get you cleaned up and make you feel better now that you've been punished."

"Yes, Master Derek." She sniffed and let the older man help her to her feet and fix her clothes.

He patted her backside and then tapped a fingertip to his cheek. Maddie obediently went on tiptoes to give Derek a kiss where he'd indicated, and pride swelled Reid's heart as he heard her whisper, "Thank you, Master Derek."

"You're very welcome, little girl. Now go say thank you to Jagger and Lawson too."

Reid watched as his still-teary Little girl gave the men her thanks, his hands itching to hold her. The stable master gave her a hug, and the chief of security patted her on the head, and he could see how she got lighter with every little bit of affection and approval.

Maddie had been through a lot today and she was a sensitive little thing. She was going to need a whole lot of comfort and cuddles and spoiling now that she'd done her penance, and he planned to give it to her. Starting now.

"Come here, Maddie-girl," he told her, beckoning with his hand. It pleased him to no end that she rushed across the room and into his outstretched arms, seeking the comfort of his body.

He hugged her real tight for a few seconds, murmuring into her hair and rubbing her back, telling her what a good girl she was and how proud he was of her, what a fine job she'd done. And then, since he was sure Derek wanted his office back, or more likely wanted to go back to the big house and spend some time with Sadie, Reid scooped Maddie up and urged her legs around his waist so he could koala-carry her back to his room.

CHAPTER 17

By the time they'd reached Reid's room, she felt wrung out like a well-used kitchen sponge. Her backside hurt, she had a headache from crying so much, her eyes were puffy, her nose was runny, and her throat was sore. She was a mess.

But Reid didn't seem to mind the snot that she'd sniveled on his shoulder or that she was still hiccupping from all her weeping. No, he grabbed a blanket off the end of the bed to wrap her in then sat down with her in the big rocking chair and rocked her.

The thing was, yes, she felt like a disaster, but she also felt clean somehow. Like once the outside of her had been tidied up, she'd be sparkly and new, not like there was still some lingering stain on her soul. Except the film of sadness that was always there, but that was just a fact of life.

It had been nice to listen to Reid's soft praises as she settled down. How he told her the slate was wiped clean, all was forgiven. That she was Daddy's good girl. She could've been upset that he talked to her in the same tones he used with the horses, but she wasn't. She could totally see why they liked it.

A MEMORABLE LITTLE MEMORIAL DAY

"You ready for a bath now, Maddie-girl?"

The sweetly murmured offer felt like it lanced straight through her rib cage to her heart. She shook her head against Reid's shoulder. Not because she didn't want him to bathe her—having his thick fingers work shampoo into her hair would be heaven—but because she was suddenly embarrassed.

"Oh, you don't have to do that," she said, trying to scoot back off his lap. "I'll just go take a shower and clean up."

But he didn't let her go.

"I don't have to do anything, little girl. But I'm your Daddy and Daddies take care of their Little girls. You've had a real rough day, and you need some comfort. I'm not happy that you wandered off, but you accepted your punishment, and it's over now. I'm real proud of how you handled your discipline. I know that was hard for you. Just as you get your hide tanned for misbehaving, you also get rewarded when you're a good girl. That's how this works."

He tilted her chin up with his thumb so she had to look at him, and she couldn't help but skim fingers over the stubble that was already darkening his jaw. The corner of Reid's mouth turned up.

"You trying to tell me I need to shave again, darlin'?"

Maddie shook her head again. She'd never tell her Daddy what to do, unless he asked or it was really, really important to her. Besides, that hadn't been what she was trying to say at all.

"No, Daddy. I...I like it. I like how you feel rough and big and strong. I like how it makes me feel."

"And how does it make you feel?" he asked, voice soft but intense, just like the expression on his face. He was always so focused on her. Made her feel so special but also kind of self-conscious. Why would a man like him pay so much attention to a girl like her?

"Soft," she offered. "Little."

"That's just how I like you, Maddie-girl. Now let's get you into that tub. No more arguments, or I'll put you over my knee again."

Well, a bath did sound much nicer than another spanking on her burning butt.

"Yes, Daddy."

* * *

He hated having to get Maddie out of the bath. She was just too damn cute with all her bubbles and the soft sighs she made when he'd washed her hair, the shade of pink her cheeks had turned when he'd soaped up her breasts and between her legs.

But the water was cooling off, and he wasn't going to have his Little girl getting chilly. That wouldn't do at all.

"Come on, Miss Pinky Prunes, time to get out of this tub."

"Do I have to?"

"Yes, but I promise I'll give you a bath again tomorrow if you're a good girl."

Her pink mouth twisted to the side, and a brief look of concern twisted her features, but then she nodded her agreement. "Okay, Daddy."

"That's a good girl."

Reid grabbed one of the big plush towels and helped Maddie out of the cooling water then wiped the stray bubbles from her skin as he toweled her off. She really was a tiny little thing, and he made a note to have her eat more at meals. Girl could use some more meat on her bones, and not just so there was more backside for him to spank.

She seemed surprised when he set her on the counter to comb out her hair and blow it dry, but the evening air could be cool here, and what kind of Daddy left his Little girl with a wet head? This may be a temporary gig, but dammit, he'd do it well.

"You have a choice now, darlin'," he told her once he'd finished and her hair slipped over her shoulders like russet silk. She was still wrapped in the towel and perched on the counter, swinging her feet gently.

Her brows creased in consternation, and he wanted to laugh. This Little girl did not like choices. But hopefully she wouldn't mind this one so much, and he wasn't going to go forward without her go-ahead.

"What is it?"

"Well, I can fetch some pajamas from your room and get you ready for bed, or..."

"Or?"

No matter how much he'd struggled living and working on his family's ranch, no matter how itchy and restless he could feel when he was ready to move on from a town, one thing he could always count on was that looking up at the big open Montana skies would clear his head.

Even if Maddie might be feeling a little off-balance and uncertain, he wasn't. Looking at her sky-blue eyes and her rosy cheeks made him feel as calm and steady as watching puffy clouds roll through on a sunny day.

"Or there's more reward to be had, if you want it."

"Oh." She nibbled on her bottom lip, and he watched the wheels turn in her head. "What kind of reward?"

He set his hands on either side of her thighs and leaned

in closer. Almost close enough to kiss that plush mouth of hers.

"A sexy kind of reward."

"Oh!"

He'd startled her, and the cords in his neck strained as he swallowed his laugh.

"Up to you," he told her and meant every single word of it. He might as well set his pants on fire if he said he wasn't aching for her, though.

He wasn't used to women thinking so hard about whether they wanted to fall into bed with him. Maybe he should've been insulted that Maddie looked so damned boggled, but he wasn't. Just curious.

What was holding up her decision? Had he done something to make her feel like *no thank you* wasn't an option? His stomach roiled at the thought. Yeah, he'd been domineering in some ways, but he'd always felt like he'd had Maddie's consent, her buy-in. If he hadn't?

"Hey," he said, nudging her chin up with a knuckle. "I maybe should've asked you this before, like when you had all your clothes on. And if I've done anything to make you feel like you're obligated to—"

Maddie shook her head. "No, it's not that. I know I can always use my safeword and you'll respect it. Or just say no since we're not playing right now. It's just..."

She huffed a sigh and rubbed a hand over her face.

"It's been a long time since I was with anyone like that, and I—"

One of those waves of sadness swept over her features as she snapped her mouth shut. He didn't feel like he could demand she spill all her secrets to him just yet, even if he wanted to, so he just waited.

A MEMORABLE LITTLE MEMORIAL DAY

* * *

HER BODY WAS VERY MUCH in favor of getting a sexy reward from Reid. At this rate, she was going to leave a certain kind of wet spot on the towel because she was getting so aroused. Thinking about his firm lips traveling over her body, imagining what the erection she could see outlined in his jeans would look like without the barrier of denim. What it would feel like, in her hand, maybe in her mouth, and most tempting of all, in her pussy... Her body was ready.

Her heart, on the other hand...

It wasn't fair to Reid. Or maybe it didn't matter. Their arrangement was only valid while they were both at the Ranch, that's what Master Derek had said. And Reid hadn't seemed in any rush to argue about that. In fact, Reid seemed like the kind of man who could have any woman he wanted and then ride off alone into the sunset.

So maybe it was okay that her body was desperate but her heart wasn't in it. Because her heart was still back in Penshaw. Maybe Reid wouldn't care because goodness knew where his heart was. He'd been kind to her, looked after her, and disciplined her, but that didn't have to mean his feelings for her were anywhere in the vicinity of love.

"I'm worried I forgot," she finished, her excuse sounding feeble to her own ears.

Reid blinked, his narrowed eyes and puckered chin with that horribly gorgeous dimple in the middle painting the very picture of perplexed, before his expression melted into a grin that had her pressing her thighs together.

"Well, if that's all that's stopping you, I'm more than happy to remind you. Discipline isn't the only lesson Daddies should teach their Little girls."

CHAPTER 18

She'd hardly said okay when Reid picked her up from the counter and hauled her over to the bed, tossed her on the mattress, and prowled over her.

Maddie barely had time to catch her breath before his firm lips were pressing against hers and she melted underneath him. Oh, his kiss was sweet. No, *sweet* was the wrong word. It was gentle but insistent, and she yielded to it just like she did to the rest of him.

He kissed her for a while, threading his fingers into her hair and holding her face, letting her rock her hips against his pelvis through his jeans. They were both panting when he finally rolled off her. Her mouth felt kiss swollen, her breasts ached, and she was certain she was soaking wet.

"Spread your legs for Daddy. Come on, be a good girl now."

Slowly, she parted her thighs, and Reid patted her mons in a way that should have been mortifying but actually made her bite her tongue so she wouldn't moan.

"There you go, that's my sweet, obedient Maddie-girl."

Her chest filled with warmth as she felt her nipples

harden, and she couldn't hold back her gasp when he parted her labia with a finger and coasted over her clit.

"Oh, someone likes their little clitty touched, hmm?"

Mortified heat flooded her face, and Maddie tried to snap her knees closed, but Reid stopped her with a growl.

"Don't you dare, you naughty thing. Now spread those legs nice and wide for Daddy."

Embarrassment warred with lust as she scooted her feet back to where they'd been.

"Uh-uh," Reid admonished with a shake of his head. "Wider than that."

It was so totally horrifying to feel the air kiss her exposed core as she obeyed her Daddy, but it also ratcheted her arousal so high she thought she could come from just another glancing touch of her clit.

What she got instead was a sharp tap between her splayed thighs that made her cry out. Had her brain feeling like she'd been electrocuted.

"That's what happens when Little girls try to hide their pretty pussies from their Daddies," he told her. "Their pussies get spanked."

Oh god. She was going to die. Of humiliation or horniness, she couldn't tell, but it was definitely going to happen.

"Now, where were we?"

With her clit still stinging and alive, she couldn't help but moan when he brushed a finger over the sensitive bud this time. If he'd spent any time toying with her, her climax probably would've gone off like an atom bomb. As things were, he continued back to her entrance, and she felt his hum of pleasure vibrate through his chest and into hers.

"Mmm, you're soaking wet, darlin'. So slick and warm."

He gathered some of her moisture then slicked his

finger back to her clit and circled it for a few seconds before sliding back to her entrance and teasing her there.

She reached up to sift her hands through his jet-black hair, but he tsked at her.

"I don't think so, Maddie-girl. Hands over your head. That's it, that's my good girl," he praised as she did what she was told.

She wasn't at all surprised when he gripped both her wrists in one of his big hands and held her down, pressing her into the mattress. She was a bit taken aback when he ordered her to spread her legs again.

"Come on, darlin'. As far as they'll go. How is Daddy supposed to finger-fuck you good and proper if you don't open that pussy up for me?"

Her back arched as he slid two fingers into her, and she closed her eyes when two became three.

For a second, though, her brain stuttered because it wasn't Reid she saw in her mind's eye but Josh. And while she didn't think Reid took sex all that seriously, she didn't think he was so unaffected by it that he'd appreciate her thinking about another man while he got her off.

She forced herself to cut the bittersweet reverie short and open her eyes to look at the man who was giving her such pleasure. And was treated to the sight of Reid dipping his head to close his mouth around her nipple and suck.

Between the restraint and the driving of his fingers and the draw on her breast, it was only a few beats before her muscles tightened around Reid's relentless fingers and she felt the swell of her arousal about to crest into a climax. Reid must've been able to tell because he thrust harder inside her to a place that made her see stars.

* * *

A MEMORABLE LITTLE MEMORIAL DAY

Goddamn, Maddie was gorgeous when she came. He wanted to make her come again and again and again. But he'd settle for just once more right now. Then as many times as he could manage between tonight and Tuesday morning.

The way she was looking at him, all big eyes and orgasm-flushed cheeks, made his head swell so big he felt like he might float away.

"Seems like you remember just fine," he teased and tapped the tip of her nose, which made her giggle.

"Yes, Daddy. Sure seems that way," she conceded, her flush deepening.

He kissed her forehead and cuddled her against him, loving the way she sculpted her body around his. Sweet little thing.

While he was dying to be inside her, he also knew Maddie needed her rest. It had been a damn rough evening for her, and she was probably tuckered out. His dick was not happy about that idea, but his dick could take a back seat because Daddy was driving.

He was about to give her an extra squeeze and tell her it was time to get her ready for bed when he felt her little hand drift from where it had been resting on his chest down to the waistband of his jeans. Shit.

"Um, Daddy?"

"Yeah, darlin'?"

It was getting real hard to keep his breathing steady when her fingers danced over his belt buckle like that. Did she know what she was doing or was she just aimlessly tinkering with the engraved silver?

"Did I do something wrong?"

He turned to get a better look at her. "No, Maddie-girl.

'Course not. You're perfect as perfect could be. What gave you the idea you'd done something wrong?"

"Well, you didn't... You haven't... It seems like I turn you on, but..."

Ah. Well, that was one worry of hers he could put to bed quick, fast, and in a hurry. Well, not that fast, hopefully.

"I don't want to hear another word out of your mouth, little girl. I'm so hard for you right now I could probably pound nails with my cock."

She giggled as he'd meant her to, and he grinned back.

"I was worried you were too tuckered out for anything else, but I'll be more than happy to make it very clear just how sexy I think you are. Is that what you want?" he asked, rolling them so he was on top of her then grinding his hips between her thighs so she could feel the thick rod of his erection against her pretty little pussy.

"Yes, Daddy."

"Oh really? Is that how you ask Daddy nicely for what you want? I thought you had better manners than that, little girl."

His smile would tell her he was teasing, but goddamn if he didn't want to hear her ask. Beg.

"Please, Daddy?" she asked, blinking up at him through thick lashes, and then slid her hand lower until she was palming his dick in a move that made his breath catch. What a little minx. "Please? I want you inside me."

"Where, babygirl? Tell Daddy where. You can use naughty words, and you won't get in trouble right now. Daddy likes it when you talk dirty during sexy times."

Maddie rolled her lips between her teeth, the picture of innocence. She killed him with her pretty face and her sweet voice, knowing her body was built for sin.

"Please, Daddy. Fuck me with your big, hard cock. I want you inside my pussy, Daddy. Please, please, please!"

Well, he wasn't in the business of denying Little girls pleasure they'd earned with their submission.

"Alright, alright. Get my pants undone and stroke me. Get me ready to claim that sweet pussy of yours, little girl."

Not that he needed the help—he was hard as hell for her already—but he wanted to feel her soft hand around his dick, torture himself a little with her gentle touch.

Maddie did what she was told and was caressing him in no time. His eyes rolled back in his head, and he groaned his pleasure, couldn't handle it for more than a couple minutes. Then he was up, stripping off the rest of his clothes before setting on her again. Kissing her again, tasting her again.

"If I take you from behind, can you come again?"

It was cute that she blushed so hard, cheeks as red as a Montana sunrise.

"Yes, Daddy. But I..."

"Do you need something? You need me to play with that pretty little clit of yours while I mount you?"

Her teeth sunk into her bottom lip, and she nodded. He could do that.

It was easy to flip her onto her tummy and get her hips in the air, chest still on the bed and her hands stretched back by her ankles. Perfect spread-out Little girl with a bright red bottom.

He grabbed a condom and rolled the latex down his length, glad his hands were steady when he couldn't wait to bury his cock in his Little girl. Notching the head of his dick at her entrance, he angled himself so he'd be able to slide right into her hot, welcoming pussy.

"Alright, Maddie-girl. Daddy's coming."

He thrust inside her, and she was hotter and slicker than he'd imagined she'd be. And the sound she made when he penetrated her was music to his ears. He couldn't imagine a heaven better than this.

Grabbing her wrists, he stroked in and out, snapping his hips against her bottom and making her mewl and whimper, hopefully from that perfect mix of pleasure and pain that seemed so intoxicating to most of the S types he'd had the fortune to know. The pitch and volume of her cries went up, and he wondered if she'd be able to come without him playing with her clit.

That experiment would have to wait for another day because there was no way he could hold off his own climax long enough to find out. So he let go of her wrist and snaked his hand between her thighs, found that little bundle of nerves, and stroked.

Maddie was rocking her hips back against him now, meeting him thrust for thrust, and chanting under her breath, "Please, Daddy, please, please, please!"

"Yes, darlin', come on. Come for Daddy. I want to feel you."

It only took a couple more strokes before Maddie was crying out, and he felt her internal muscles clamp down on his dick. The pulse of her around him set off his own orgasm, and he lost his rhythm as his balls tightened and he spilled inside her.

CHAPTER 19

A few days later, someone was shaking her awake in her nice warm bed. That was mean.

"Psst, Maddie!"

Ugh, was it really Sunday morning already? Couldn't be, she felt like she'd barely gone to sleep.

"Maddie!"

Why was Tamsyn whispering if it was morning? None of this made any sense. It didn't make any more sense when she peeled her eyes open to a dark room, her roommate looming over her.

"Get up," Tamysn said, a mischievous smile on her face and her eyes twinkling in the low light of her phone screen. A screen that said it was two o'clock in the morning. What the heck?

"For what?" Maddie grumbled, feeling as though half her brain were still asleep.

"It's a tradition!"

That's when Maddie noticed Tamsyn wasn't alone. There were a few other Littles behind her, and they were all whispering and tittering amongst themselves. She recognized the one who had announced that whatever she was supposed to crowbar herself out of bed for was "a tradition" as Sadie, the woman who'd greeted them when they arrived at the Ranch.

"What's a tradition?"

"It's called the red, white, and blue swim, and we do it every Memorial Day week. I have to change the days though so Daddy doesn't see it coming. Sometimes we do it before, sometimes we do it after. Once we even did it on Memorial Day itself."

Maddie shot Sadie a skeptical look. From what she knew of Master Derek, it would take more than a shift of a few days on a calendar to fool the man.

"Is this one of your pranks?"

Sadie's mouth twisted to the side. "I wouldn't call it so much of a prank as a..."

"Tradition?" Maddie supplied.

"Yes, exactly. So get up, we've got to go!"

She'd heard all about Sadie's pranks and the other monkey business the Littles got up to around here. She'd also heard about the spankings they got for their antics. Since her butt was still sore from her punishment the other day, she didn't think she wanted to risk it, even if Sadie claimed it was a tradition and not a prank.

"Um, no thanks. I don't think Reid would like it. I already got in enough trouble this week."

Sadie pouted. "Come on, Maddie. You have to participate in some shenanigans while you're at the Ranch. It's basically required. I wouldn't feel like I had done my job as hostess if you didn't have at least a little naughty fun."

Maddie was glad for the darkness because her face was probably the shade of a lobster. She and Reid had had plenty of naughty fun so far, and she expected there would be more to come before they went their separate ways on Tuesday morning.

"Really, I'm good. Tamsyn can have my share of the naughty fun. I'll just go back to sleep."

Sadie's pout deepened, and she crossed her arms over her chest. Why was she wearing a bathrobe? This was all very confusing. Before she could attempt to cajole Maddie into joining their caper, Tamsyn rested a hand on her shoulder.

"Give me a sec?" she asked the brunette who was far too perky for two a.m.

"Okay," Sadie agreed. "But only a sec because we've got to get started."

Once Sadie had turned back to the excited knot of Littles behind her, Tamsyn plopped on the bed next to Maddie.

"I know Reid already spanked you a few days ago for wandering off and you don't want to get in trouble again. But—"

Maddie rolled her eyes. It was easy for Tamsyn to say *but* when her butt wasn't going to be the one getting blistered if they got caught doing whatever this so-called tradition was.

"But part of being a Little is not always making the best decisions. Littles are *supposed* to get up to some mischief. From what Sadie told me, we'll probably get scolded but not really in trouble. So come on, Maddie. Please? For me? You've been spending so much time with Reid that we haven't had enough time to make memories."

Oh, she was going to pull this guilt trip?

"That's not even fair! You're the one who told me to find a Daddy!"

Tamsyn smirked at her. "I like to have my cake and eat it too. Now come on, I already got out your bathing suit..."

* * *

"Do they really think they're being quiet?"

Derek shook his head and smiled indulgently. "Probably."

There were about twenty Littles splashing around in the outdoor pool, and there was a whole lot of giggling and flailing going on. It was too cute for words.

Reid had been confused when Derek had called him earlier in the day to tell him the Littles were going to pull a "prank" tonight and that the Bigs were supposed to "catch" them.

"If you know it's happening, why are you letting them get away with it?" he'd asked.

He knew Derek loved his wife to the ends of the earth and back, but he also knew the man didn't care for any of Sadie's capers that would make the Ranch look bad.

"On the scale of Sadie's pranks, it's pretty harmless. I'd rather she be planning her red, white, and blue swim than cooking up something that would actually cause trouble."

Reid could see what he meant now. The Littles had started by dipping into a few of the Jacuzzi tubs that bordered the pool area, and then they ran inside to horse around in the indoor pool. Their last stop was the outdoor pool, which was heated but not enough to make it warm on a May evening in Montana. Some teeth had already started chattering, and it occurred to Reid why they called it the red, white, and blue swim—because they went from the hottest water to the coldest, with the indoor pool in between. Silly but clever Littles.

A MEMORABLE LITTLE MEMORIAL DAY

"It's just about time for us to play our parts, everyone," Derek announced to the Bigs who were standing around. "Don't forget to pretend to be mad."

Everyone laughed and shook their heads. The things they did for their Littles. But Reid wouldn't trade this night for anything.

He'd been pleased to see Maddie joining in the fun, letting loose, and looking like she was having a genuinely good time. Giggling and squealing along with the rest of the Littles as they jumped into pools and clambered out, skittered along hallways while wrapped in their bathrobes but still dripping wet, and shushing each other loud enough to wake the dead.

Of course, since Derek knew this was happening, he'd alerted all the Bigs and had a couple lifeguards on hand in case anything went sideways. You'd think the Littles would notice their group—they'd hidden in darkened rooms to keep an eye on the Jacuzzi hijinks and now, and in the office of the lifeguards, which faced the indoor pool—but they were probably having too much fun and thinking they were super stealthy to pay too much attention. Cuties.

He was almost sad to interrupt their fun, but even from here he could see a bunch of the Littles were looking chilly—they probably had goose bumps and blue lips but were too delighted with themselves to care too much. Well, he cared. He wouldn't have Maddie catching a chill even if he loved to see her cavorting around like she didn't have a care in the world.

Derek swung open the door to the patio, and his big, booming voice echoed in the crisp night air as he bellowed, "Sadie Marie Hawkins, you are in a world of trouble!"

Then all hell broke loose.

* * *

OH NO, they'd been caught! All around her, Littles were shrieking and splashing and sloshing. Maddie's own heart had gone into overdrive and was pounding away in her chest. She hated getting in trouble, *hated* it.

Why had she let Sadie and Tamsyn talk her into this? She was a good girl and now Reid was going to be so mad. Yes, she'd get her bottom spanked again, but she hated disappointing him way more than she hated getting her butt paddled.

Except that when she looked around at the legion of Bigs storming the pool deck, most of them were smiling. Or trying not to smile. Only a few of them looked actually angry, and she was pretty sure that was just because they were good at acting.

She couldn't help but scan the horde for her Daddy, and it didn't take long for her to find Reid who gave her one of those swoon-worthy crooked smiles and a wink before he called, "Madigan Rose Arsenault, what are you doing out of bed at this hour? And in a pool! You're gonna catch your death, little girl."

She swam over to the edge of the pool and climbed out, her skin breaking out in gooseflesh as soon as it hit the air.

"Sorry, Daddy."

"Oh, you're gonna be sorry. Where's your robe?"

She pointed to the pile of terry cloth on the nearest lounger, and Reid grabbed it then shook it out before wrapping it around her and chafing her limbs.

Most of the Littles had been caught by now. Indeed, some of them were already over their Bigs' knees with their bathing suits pulled down or, in the case of those who'd worn one-pieces, pulled up between their butt cheeks.

A MEMORABLE LITTLE MEMORIAL DAY

They were getting spanked right here, on the pool deck, in front of everyone. How humiliating.

Maddie looked at Reid imploringly. She'd obey if he told her to get herself over his lap out here, but she really didn't like being scolded in front of other people. She needn't have worried. Before she knew what was happening, Reid had tossed her over his shoulder and was heading into the main building.

"Arm okay, Maddie-girl?" he asked, just loud enough for her to hear.

"Uh-huh," she responded, and then her robe was flung over her back and her Daddy landed a harsh spank on her still-wet butt cheek.

The sharp sting made her yelp. "Ow!"

Maybe she wasn't in real trouble—Reid would never wink at her if he were really mad—but she was definitely going to get a spanking. It was kind of fun to squirm and fuss while he carried her down the hall to his room. Once they were inside, he set her on her feet and looked her up and down.

"Let's get you outta this wet swimsuit and into a hot shower," he said, clearly not expecting a response since he'd already circled a hand around her wrist and was towing her to the bathroom.

It finally occurred to her to ask, "Do you know what happened to Tamsyn? Did she get in trouble too? She doesn't have a Daddy to punish her."

"Are you worried about your friend getting spanked or not getting spanked?" Reid asked, dark brow quirking.

"Both," she admitted, and Reid chuckled.

"Well, there's a reason Fitz isn't here. He volunteered to spank your friend since Derek and Nanny J already have their hands full with unaccompanied Littles. They went to your room."

Oh. That was unexpected. Fitz and Tamsyn? Really? She hadn't seen that coming. When the four of them had hung out or had meals together, those two had seemed more like peers than Daddy and Middle, but maybe behind closed doors, the dynamic shifted.

"Now don't get all excited, I can see those wheels turning in your head. You're as bad as Derek. Tamsyn and Fitz are friends, and they're just playing around. Besides, I don't think either of them wanted to be here for what I'm about to do to you, little girl."

CHAPTER 20

After getting her warm, soaping her up from head to toe, and washing the chlorine out of her hair, he took his flush-faced Little out to the main room of the suite and set her over his lap on the couch.

Her backside had some bruising from her punishment the other day, but it wasn't anything serious. He'd go real easy on her since spanking an already-bruised bottom would be plenty painful for what he had in mind.

Rubbing the soft skin of her buttocks, he talked to her.

"This isn't a punishment like you got for wandering off and not telling anyone where you were headed. That was real discipline, and I was making a point. You did disobey the rules by being out of bed at this hour, and you shouldn't have been in the water unsupervised. But since this is a tradition and everyone was in on it—"

His Little girl squawked in indignation. "You *knew?*"

"Sure did, darlin', which is good news for your backside."

Her fit of pique was over real quick, more funny than anything else.

"Anyway, since you were never in any danger and because I was happy to see you letting loose and enjoying yourself with your friends, you're only getting a little spanking. Not a good-girl spanking, but more like…"

"Funishment?" she offered, peeking over her shoulder.

He chuckled at the silly word but nodded. "That's a good way to describe it. So you let me know if it starts to feel like a real naughty-girl punishment, okay? You've got some bruising, so it might hurt more than I intend."

She nodded, accepting. Such an obliging little thing. It was fun to tame brats sometimes, but he found it exhausting after a while. He had a hard time imagining tiring of his pliant, trusting Maddie-girl.

He stroked her for another minute and then raised his hand and brought it down on her upturned backside. The connection between his palm and Maddie's flesh was electric, even when it was mild. He had to hold himself back from tossing her on the bed and having his way with her. Not yet.

Under his hand, her skin warmed and pinked up. Reid loved her gasps and squeaks and whimpers, and he tried to calibrate how she was feeling today against when he'd spanked her before. The punishment she'd gotten the other day had definitely made her more tender, but she was still pretty tough.

Once he had her worked up as hard as he was willing to go tonight, he started in on his lecture. It wouldn't be long, but he did want to remind her that some of her behavior tonight would get her punished for real in the future. The future being the next two days and change.

That didn't seem right. Not at all. The thought of leaving here and never seeing Maddie again knotted his stomach and not in a good-nervous, keyed-up way. No, he didn't like to think about losing her. Which was odd given that this was already longer than 80 percent of his relationships and he'd spent more time with Maddie than he had with probably 90 percent of the women he'd dated. But what choice did he have?

The irritating little Fitz perched on his shoulder said he might not have a choice but he could at least try. Well, Fitz could shut up.

"Sneaking out of your room in the middle of the night is against the rules. The rules of the Ranch and my rules. If you sneak out again, you won't be getting funishment. You understand, little girl? Won't just be my hand either. I take your safety very seriously. How am I supposed to keep you safe if you're wandering around at all hours? Not acceptable. Promise me that won't happen again."

Maddie whimpered because he'd been bringing his palm down on the same spot on her backside over and over again. Not any harder, but he knew the impact would feel harder with the repetition. Neat lazy Top trick that was.

"I—I promise, Daddy. I won't sneak out again. Swear. I'm sorry. I'm s-sorry."

He switched cheeks to make his other point.

"I know you're a good swimmer, but you and the other Littles still shouldn't have been in the water unsupervised. Even the very best swimmers need help sometimes, and there can be accidents. So never, ever again are you to be in the water without an adult around, preferably a lifeguard. You want to go swimming with your friends and there's no one around, you call me and I'll come. I'd rather drop whatever I'm doing than have you get hurt. Tell me you understand."

"I understand, D-Daddy," she choked out, sounding like she was close to crying. Had he pushed her too far? He hadn't meant for her to take this as an actual punishment. "I won't ever go in the water unsupervised ever again. I'm sorry I put myself in danger."

"There you go," he soothed, rubbing the skin he'd just been smacking.

The heat between them felt deeper than the surface friction. He felt like he had a chemistry, an understanding with Maddie that he'd never known with anyone else. And wasn't that a crying shame?

He bent over his Little girl, still caressing her bottom.

"Y'okay, darlin'? I wasn't aiming to make you cry. This is supposed to be fun."

"I know," she said in a voice barely above a whisper. "But I still feel bad. I did misbehave, and I did break the rules, and I did it without knowing you were right there."

He hummed his understanding. "So you feel like you deserve a punishment?"

Maddie tensed over his lap and then sighed. "Yes, Sir."

"Ah," he said, applying a swat to her sit spot. "No *Sir* here."

"Yes, Daddy. Sorry, Daddy."

"That's okay, I know you feel guilty, and it's hard to feel worthy of Daddy's love when you feel like you messed up, isn't it?"

There was a pause during which he realized what he'd said and apparently so had she.

"Yes, Daddy," she croaked after a beat, sounding as though she would burst into tears any second.

"But I've got news for you, little girl. You're always worthy of Daddy's love. I may not always love your behavior and I'll discipline you accordingly, but Daddy always loves you. Breaking the rules might be naughty but you're never a bad girl. You're always Daddy's good girl, and punishments just help wipe away the tarnish of misbehavior. I never ever expect you to be perfect, darlin'. But I do expect you to accept the discipline I mete out with humility and grace. I also expect you to know that no matter what you've done, deep down you always have Daddy's love. Say it back to me so I know you understand."

Oh, those sniffles broke his heart. What a tenderhearted Little girl. In addition to the familiar warmth he felt for Maddie, there was a stab of guilt in his own chest.

What business did he have saying Daddy would always love her? Even if that were true, was he going to be around to prove that day in and day out? How could he when she lived in Ohio and he lived out here and they'd both been acting like this was an assignment for the week? It didn't feel like an assignment anymore. It maybe even felt like the love he was professing. Sure, if Maddie put herself in danger, he'd lose his goddamn mind, but he'd forgive her any damn thing. In her heart, she was a good girl, and that's all that mattered to him.

Everyone screwed up—god knew he did, and Littles probably did more than most—but that didn't make her unworthy. Just meant she needed a Daddy. The idea of anyone else filling that role made him queasy.

It wasn't fair for him to be ruminating like a damn cow on all this while he had a Little girl over his lap who needed his attention. He could save that uncomfortable introspection for later, after he'd taken care of her. After he'd relieved her of her guilt, made her feel all shiny and new and forgiven. Loved.

"Say it, Maddie-girl," he directed.

"Even when I'm not perfect, even when I misbehave, even when I'm naughty..."

Reid could almost feel the weight of Maddie's disappointment in herself weighing her down, crushing her lungs, making it near impossible to say the words. He'd help her as best he knew how, and that was by giving her an order. She might not be able to do it for herself yet, but he knew damn well his brave and dutiful Little girl would say it for him, no matter what it cost her. Submission and faith were just that hardwired into that pretty little head of hers.

"Say it, darlin', don't make your Daddy wait."

"I'm a good girl, and Daddy loves me."

Her whisper was barely audible, but the sobbing that followed was loud. Poor little thing. He couldn't bear to hear her cry like that without holding her tight and giving her some reassurance, so he turned her over and gathered her close, laying kisses on the top of her head as she wept into his shoulder.

Took a while for her to calm down enough to look at him, and when she did, her eyes were red and swollen. So much for funishment.

"Hey babygirl, you doin' okay?"

"Yes, Daddy. I'm sorry."

"What are you sorry for?"

"I asked you to punish me, and then I cried before you even started. That doesn't feel like...humility and grace," she recited.

"Your brain plays some awful mean tricks on you, darlin'. Did you tell Daddy no?"

Maddie shook her head, eyes wide.

"Did you argue with me about whether you should get a punishment or what it should be?"

"No, Daddy."

"Then I think you're doing just fine."

CHAPTER 21

Reid kissed away some of her tears and ran the backs of his knuckles down her cheek. How had she gotten so simultaneously lucky and unlucky? Lucky because he was a good man and a good Daddy, but unlucky because...he wasn't hers to keep. But for a few more days she could pretend.

"You still feeling the need for me to tan your hide, little girl?"

Would he not if she said no? But what the heck good would that do her since, despite his assurances, she still felt squished by guilt?

Yes, it had turned out to be harmless fun in the end, but she hadn't known that. She should've stuck to her guns that her Daddy wouldn't like it and not have let Sadie and Tamsyn talk her into their antics. Better to be a stick-in-the-mud than to disappoint your Daddy. Even though Reid had been insistent she hadn't. But the nagging little voice in her head wouldn't let it go, all the could-haves and what-ifs so persistent.

"Yes, Daddy. I'm sorry."

"What are you sorry for now?" he asked, a little teasing

in his tone and the way the corner of his mouth pulled up, showing off that dimple she loved.

"Is it topping from the bottom if I tell you I need to be punished?"

"No, darlin'. I want you to tell me what you need. I'll decide if that's true, but of course I want to hear your thoughts, always. I wasn't going to punish you, but I also don't want you feeling guilty, so I'm going to do whatever it takes to polish that tarnish away. I like it when you sparkle."

She liked being burnished and buffed by her Daddy until she shone, and getting her bottom spanked was one of the ways Reid did that.

Maddie smiled at him—or tried. She still felt watery and washed out, but her Daddy didn't seem to mind. Just tipped up her face with a grip on her chin and kissed her softly on the lips.

"Are you ready for your punishment now, or do you need a minute? We could even do it in the morning if you're worn out."

"I don't think I'll be able to sleep," she admitted.

"Then now it is. Hold tight for a second. I'll be right back."

Reid set her down on the couch, and she felt the absence of his warmth keenly. She was going to be frozen to her core when she had to go home to Penshaw. Especially since Tamsyn would leave a few days after they got back, and then she'd be alone except for a ghost and a grave. Would that really be enough to sustain her? Then she felt terrible for wondering. Of course it would. Had to be, without her being forced to betray the man she loved, so it would.

When Reid came back, it was with a small leather

paddle in hand. It was dark brown and beautiful in its own wicked way, and she couldn't stop staring at it.

"Pretty, isn't it?" he mused, smacking his palm with the implement. She cringed at the sound, but her stomach also flipped. Not entirely in trepidation. "Bought it at the gift shop in case you decided to press your luck. Good thing I have it on hand."

Reid sat back down on the couch and beckoned to her. "C'mere, little girl. Over my lap you get. Time to pay the piper."

Settling herself over her Daddy's knee brought both tension and relief. That evil little paddle was going to hurt like heck, but that was what she wanted, wasn't it? Pain to absolve her of wrongdoing and wipe away her shame.

Reid trapped her legs between his strong thighs and told her, "Hands, darlin'."

Maddie placed her hands at the small of her back, crossing her wrists, and Reid held them both in one of his hands.

"This is going to be hard and fast, Maddie-girl. I'm restraining you because it's going to hurt. You can squirm and buck all you want, but you're not going anywhere because Daddy's got you."

The words melted something inside her, and she knew she'd made the right choice telling Reid what she needed. Not that she was looking forward to wincing every time she sat down for the next few days, but some bruises on her butt were far preferable to lingering guilt trying to strangle her soul.

"I want to hear every squawk and squeak outta you, every cry and moan, so don't you dare try to be quiet. No cussing, though, or I'll wash your mouth out with soap."

She didn't think she'd actually enjoy getting her mouth

soaped, but the thought of it made her wet. Then again, she probably wasn't going to exactly enjoy getting her butt blistered shortly, but that would probably have her slick between her thighs too.

"Yes, Daddy."

"Alright, here we go."

When the first strike of the paddle landed on the fleshiest part of her backside, she yelped. Yes, that smarted, and she didn't even have time to properly recover from it because the thick leather was coming down on her bottom fast and hard as promised, her flesh burning from the searing swats. It *hurt*. It hurt so bad she couldn't even fully register all the pain, never mind process it.

"Ow!" she cried, wrenching her wrists against her Daddy's strong hand and kicking her feet up off the carpet, trying to tilt her hips to avoid any of the impact. But she couldn't. Reid had used his own body to bind her, and it was proving remarkably effective.

Daddy's got you.

Of course he did. It was a wonderful and horrifying realization. She knew she should tell Reid about Josh, should explain what was going on in that "busy brain" of hers, as he called it. He'd probably be really mad at her for not having told him sooner. Well, maybe not mad because it was hard for her to picture her easygoing Daddy as truly angry, but he'd be disappointed, which was maybe worse.

For now, she would just let herself cry. Partly because the spanking she was getting was maybe the most punishing she'd ever had. The paddle strokes were unbearably firm and wretchedly close together. But also because she was so conflicted and there was no paddle on this earth that could silence a conscience guilty of betraying her love.

A MEMORABLE LITTLE MEMORIAL DAY

Everything hurt. Her body, her heart. One she could fix, the other not so much.

For however loudly she screamed and however long she wailed, Reid didn't stop until she was practically choking on her sobs, so distraught she couldn't see through the tears. It took her a long moment to realize he'd stopped because the fire on her backside was so intense. Yes, she was going to remember this for a very long time.

She would've liked to scramble into his lap and throw her arms around his neck, but even when he'd released his grip on her wrists and thighs, she couldn't seem to move. Once he'd turned her over and sat her in a straddle over his lap, she clung to his neck and let the rest of the tears flow.

"You're okay, darlin'. It's all over now. Daddy's got you. I'm gonna hold my good girl all night long."

He was? They'd never spent the night together, and it hadn't bothered her exactly. He'd tucked her in with Cleopatra at bedtime, which made her feel squirmy in the best way, and he'd wake her in the morning if she wasn't already up when he came to fetch her. Spending the whole night cuddled up with him, his thick arm draped over her and holding her close, maybe waking up to his thick cock pressing against her backside though...

"Please, Daddy, please," she begged.

"Wild horses couldn't drag me away."

CHAPTER 22

Maddie snuffled and stirred in his arms. He'd let her sleep in since, on top of running around the resort and swimming in the middle of the night, she'd also taken a pretty serious spanking, cried buckets, and had basically passed out on top of him.

He'd cleaned her up as well as he could without waking her before he tucked her in, took care of a couple things, then joined her. And he'd slept better last night than he had in ages. Probably just that he was beat from all the impact play and toting his Little girl around. Must be it.

When she pressed her hips back and ground her bottom against his morning wood, he knew she was awake.

He pulled her tighter against him and kissed the sensitive spot right below her ear before nipping her lobe. "Morning, little girl."

"Morning, Daddy."

Aw, she sounded soft with leftover sleep, and it was sweet, but she also sounded happy. She rolled over to face him, wincing when her backside touched the mattress, and peered up at him.

A MEMORABLE LITTLE MEMORIAL DAY

"How did Cleopatra get here?"

The worn manatee was sandwiched between them, and Reid was a little peeved that Maddie's small tits weren't pressed into his chest instead of against her stuffie, but he'd live. Worth it to see her look at him like he'd performed a miracle.

"Where do you think Fitz spent last night? I called him and asked him to bring Cleopatra here. You were already knocked out, so I just tucked her in with you. You sleep alright?"

Maddie nodded. "Really well. I must've been so tired from...everything last night because now that I'm awake, I'm sore all over."

"I bet you are, darlin'. What do you say we have some breakfast in bed?"

"For real?"

"'Course for real. But I'm too hungry to wait for Chef Connor to cook something up, so I think I'll devour you first."

He rolled her onto her back and took Cleopatra from her hands. She relinquished the stuffie but also tracked his hand until he'd set the manatee safely on the nightstand. Did she honestly think he'd just toss Cleopatra off the bed? Not a chance.

"You too sore to be on your back?"

"No, Daddy."

The corner of his mouth tugged up. "You like it? Feeling your well-spanked behind rub on these soft sheets?"

Maddie pursed her lips. "They don't feel soft anymore."

"Well, I bet we can distract you."

It was easy to climb over her and pepper her face with kisses, make her giggle. Easier still to press his lips to hers firmly, let her know who was in charge, and it only took a brush of his tongue over the seam of her lips for her to grant him entrance. That's when the devouring started.

If he couldn't bring her back to Almandine, he wanted to consume her. Take every piece of her he possibly could with him and maybe leave her wrecked enough that she couldn't imagine being whole without him.

That was beyond selfish given the kind of man he was. If he wasn't going to play for keeps, he shouldn't set her on fire on his way out the door. Wasn't fair to her. Maddie deserved a happily ever after with a good man, and he shouldn't do anything to stand in the way of that. But that wasn't going to stop him from eating her so good she'd call out his name in her sleep and leave her new man wondering who the hell this Reid was. Yeah, he could be an asshole.

But he was an asshole who prided himself on pleasing his partners, so he'd take his time, make Maddie scream from pleasure instead of the wicked paddling he'd given her last night. Starting by moving from her mouth to her neck, licking and nipping and sucking the smooth skin there while wrapping a fist in her hair.

Sweet little thing arched under him and let out a breathy moan already.

"You like that, Maddie-girl?" he murmured between bites and kisses and savored her desperate "uh-huh" as much as he was relishing the taste of her skin.

Moving down her neck to her collarbone, the hollow of her throat, it was impossible to resist the pink-tipped mounds of her breasts. He had to love on those just as thoroughly as he had her throat and suck on her nipples until she was squirming and panting and begging. Gave the scant handfuls a few slaps each to satisfy the masochist in her, rev up her engines harder, ratchet her arousal higher.

He didn't want to let go of her hair, but if he wanted to

kiss lower on her body—and he did—he would have to. So he gave it one last wrenching tug that made her mewl, and then he was skimming his lips over her soft tummy and down to the promised land between her thighs.

"Let me in, little girl," he demanded, and Maddie complied, spreading her legs so he could fit his shoulders beneath her knees and grab her hips.

Reid held her there, digging his fingers into her flanks until she cried out, and then he dipped his head, parting her labia with his tongue so he could have access to that beautiful pink pearl that was nestled between them. He latched on to the sensitive bud with his lips, stroked it with his tongue, and even bit.

Between the way she was writhing and her desperate pleas, he couldn't imagine Maddie was too far from her climax. But he wanted to make this good. Real good, for her.

He released her hip and slid first one finger and then two inside her, found that little patch of nerves on the front wall of her pussy, and stroked her there. Those blue eyes of hers rolled back into her head when he pushed a third finger inside her. He hoped he was making her feel cracked wide open and subject to his tender mercies.

To drive the point home, he sucked her clit, and that's when she was overcome, gasping and moaning, making the most delicious sounds he'd ever heard. Thrashing under his mouth and rocking her hips into his face. It was heady to be surrounded by her this way—the taste and smell of her sex, the noises she made, the feel of her in his mouth and in his hands. She was his whole world. Then again, that wasn't news.

Reid eased her through her shuddering orgasm and didn't stop stroking her until he was sure she'd gleaned all the pleasure possible from her climax. When it was finally over, she lay limp in front of him, her hand sifting through his hair while she laughed.

"What's so funny, little girl?" he asked then kissed the creamy skin of her inner thigh.

"Nothing. Nothing is funny. That was amazing. I just... I'm..."

She interrupted herself with another giggle. Too cute for words.

He climbed over her until he could kiss the corner of her lips and then licked inside her mouth so she could taste her intoxicating flavor that lingered on his tongue.

"Mmm, maybe you're delirious from hunger."

"Maybe," she agreed, smiling at his joke.

"Lucky you, Daddy's got something to feed you before breakfast gets here."

Her eyes and mouth widened into Os.

"Mm-hmm, just like that darlin'," he told her, his dick throbbing at the sight. "Let's get you on your knees so Daddy can feed you properly."

* * *

REID TOSSED a pillow onto the ground and helped her climb down from the bed and situate herself, which made her giggle more. Apparently really good orgasms made her punch-drunk, and she vaguely remembered that from her time with Josh.

"Still laughing, Maddie-girl? Something funny now?"

"I mean, a little," she admitted.

"What is it? You gonna share with Daddy?"

He took her chin between his fingers and tilted her chin up, making her breath catch in her throat. What was it about that gesture that pressed her buttons so very hard? But he'd asked her a question, so she'd answer him. Even if she might get swatted for her response.

"It's just kind of funny that you're more than fine bruising my bottom but don't want to hurt my knees."

Her Daddy grinned back at her. "That's exactly right. Now why don't you put that mouth to better use than teasing Daddy, or I think you'll find your bottom even more bruised."

Maddie didn't bother to respond but leaned forward to lick the tip of his cock. She explored his erection—flushed to a dusky red, thick, and stiff—with her tongue and her lips. She wasn't surprised when he fisted a hand in her hair near her scalp. His groan pleased her, though—he gave her so much pleasure, and now she was able to return the favor, taking the head into her mouth and sucking on it lightly before twisting her tongue around and down the hard shaft.

He tasted musky and salty, and she closed her eyes so she could concentrate on the feel of him in her mouth.

"That's real good, Maddie-girl. You're a good little cocksucker. Now let Daddy feed some more of his cock into your throat. Don't fight it, just breathe. That's it, that's my good girl."

She took as much of him into her mouth as she could and tried to suppress her gag reflex as he fisted a second hand in her hair and pushed her face farther down on his shaft. It was disconcerting that she couldn't breathe when she'd taken so much of him into her mouth, but he only held her there for a second, then backed off, then did it again.

"Little longer this time, darlin'," he told her. "You tap my leg three times if you get scared."

She nodded as best she could, and then he was edging

back into the tight channel of her throat. Reid controlling the very air she breathed was enough to make her hum with need, and he groaned in response.

When he backed off, she noticed he was panting. She'd done that. With the thick mushroom head still on her tongue, he tipped her face up.

"Just like that. You're gonna deepthroat Daddy's cock just like that, and when I come in your mouth, you're going to swallow every last drop like the good girl you are."

Maddie licked the underside of his dick in answer, and Reid swore under his breath.

"You're gonna play with yourself too. Stroke that sweet little clit of yours and roll a nipple between your fingers. I want you coming again when I blow my load down your throat. Show me how much you like it when Daddy comes in your mouth."

It was her turn to moan desperately, and her fingers flew to do as he'd commanded. She'd been a little worried when he told her to play with herself that she wouldn't be able to come again, but that was not going to be an issue. If anything, it might be hard to hold herself off until he spilled inside her.

Once she'd started rubbing circles over her swollen, needy clit and playing with her taut nipple, Reid rocked his pelvis to push more of his cock over her tongue. Started out slow and steady but increased the depth and the pace until her face was getting fucked. It was scary for a second until she heard him murmur, "Don't fight it, little girl. Just let Daddy use your mouth. Surrender. That's it, what a good girl."

Flicking the off switch to her brain was so easy in some ways and hard in others. Right now it was easy, her body and brain flooded with all the good chemicals and still blissed out after her initial climax. And now she was certain she'd be having another in short order.

"Come on, Maddie-girl. Daddy's almost there. Pinch that greedy little clit of yours, tug that nipple real hard. There you go. Daddy's darlin' likes it a little rough, I know."

Maddie followed his directions as though in a trance and let all the sensations wash over her. Her Daddy's pure dominance as he fucked her throat and pulled her hair, the exhilarating pleasure-pain he was forcing her to inflict upon herself. It was so, so much, and it was getting near impossible to hold off her orgasm. She was so grateful when the rhythm of Reid's hips changed, and he ground out, "Now, babygirl, now. Come for Daddy now."

She felt the first spurt of his release in her throat, and that triggered her own climax. As Reid emptied himself into her mouth, her body pulsed and shuddered, all her muscles squeezing and letting go until she thought she wouldn't be able to hold herself together anymore.

Thankfully, Reid's grip at her scalp kept her upright and when she'd sucked him dry, he tugged her up from the floor only to flop side by side with him on the bed and cuddle. They were silent for a few minutes as their breathing settled, and then her Daddy planted a kiss on the top of her head.

"Now, what does my little girl want for actual breakfast?"

CHAPTER 23

Memorial Day had finally come to the Ranch, the last day before Maddie went home to Penshaw and he headed back to Almandine. They had spent the better part of yesterday in bed except for their customary trail ride, and Maddie had joined Tamsyn and the other Littles for a tea party.

They'd had a great time this week, and that was what they'd both come here for. Or rather, that's what their stubborn-ass friends had dragged them here for. Mission accomplished, and leaving shouldn't be a problem.

So why did he feel sick about it, and had since he'd woken up with her yesterday morning?

Fitz had kept his big mouth shut for the drive out to the river Derek told him had the best fly-fishing this time of year, but Reid didn't expect his friend's silence to last forever. There was a reason for that; he'd known this man to mess in other people's affairs for eighteen years, and he supposed he ought to be grateful it'd taken Fitz this long to really sniff around in his.

"So what's going to happen between you and Maddie after tomorrow?"

Reid shrugged. "Dunno. Probably nothing."

If his eyebrows were to believed, Fitz had some capital-T thoughts about that.

"Really? Because you two seem pretty serious."

"How serious can people get in eight days?" he muttered, feeling salty as all hell.

"I don't know, why don't you tell me?" Fitz asked, echoing the thoughts that were churning in Reid's skull like rapids.

If he was being honest, this was the most serious he'd ever felt about a woman, by a mile. A hundred miles.

Reid shrugged. "Doesn't matter. I live here; she lives in Ohio. I'm not really the long-distance type."

"You could be."

It would be real great if his friend and his own thoughts didn't agree on so much. Make it easier to tell Fitz to shut the hell up and fish.

"You know me. A woman can barely keep my attention if she's right in front of my face, never mind one who's fifteen hundred miles away. There's a pretty good chance I'd fuck that up quick, fast, and in a hurry, and it doesn't feel right to put her in that position. Maddie's a good girl, one who really needs a Daddy who will be there for her, who will keep his promises. Not some fuckboy who's gonna love her and leave her like some bad country song."

Fitz looked over, hands frozen on his reel, an expression of "what kind of dumbass are you" on his face. Reid wanted to tell him he was the usual kind of dumbass.

"Why are you looking at me like that?"

Fitz shook his head and then recast. Was the asshole going to explain himself or not?

"First of all, you've already fucked her, right?"

Irritation made Reid feel all spiky. He hadn't *fucked*

Maddie. Not that there was anything wrong with fucking. He loved to fuck, and Maddie seemed like a girl who could enjoy hard and rough just as well as slow and sweet. She had this aura around her that said she enjoyed flesh and sweat and all the things bodies could do—she just needed someone to make her feel safe enough to do it. Hell, they'd gotten pretty filthy yesterday.

"We were physically intimate, yes."

Out of the corner of his eye, he saw the surprise splattered all over his buddy's face. Before he could grumble in his direction, Fitz shook his head and cleared the expression.

"So you've already loved her. And if you don't pursue this beyond when we head home after the farewell brunch tomorrow, you will have...?"

"Fuck you," Reid muttered. But his friend wasn't wrong. He was already near doing the thing he didn't want to do. "But if we just go our separate ways after this is over, it was just a vacation fling, you know? No promises, no commitments, just a fun story to share with her friends over cosmos or whatever girls drink these days. That time she fucked a cowboy."

Truth be told, though, he couldn't imagine Maddie sitting in a bar, gossiping about a man she'd had a holiday indulgence with. And it got under his skin to think of her telling that story only to come home to an empty bed afterward.

Maddie deserved to come home to a man who loved her and looked after her. Who would help her overcome her fears and who would play games with her—both things like Connect Four, but also, if she wanted the rush of going home with a stranger but the security of being with someone she loved, someone who would meet her at a hotel bar and pretend to seduce her.

Made him feel like he had a pebble in his boot to think of her doing that with anyone but him.

Fitz raised one of his eyebrows, that nosy ginger bastard. "Nothing wrong with that. If that's what you want."

They were silent for a few minutes, enjoying the cold rush of the river around them tempered by the warm air. It was really a perfect day. The only thing Reid could imagine making it better was having Maddie tucked in front of him so he could show her how to reel the line in and cast off again. And when she got tired of fishing lessons, she could sun herself on a blanket on the shore. Read a book while she munched on some snacks or maybe took a nap because being outside could make Little girls sleepy.

His daydreaming was interrupted by Fitz.

"Lemme ask you something. When's the last time you quit your job?"

Reid had to think about that. It'd been a while. And truthfully, he'd probably stay at Mason's until he had enough money and experience to start his own shop.

"Dunno, maybe six years ago."

"And how many jobs did you quit before that?"

He laughed. "I don't think I can count that high."

"I don't think you can either," Fitz joked. "And how long have we been friends—best friends if you wanna get sappy about it?"

"Maybe eighteen years?"

Reid couldn't remember quite when it had happened, but he knew Fitz had been in his life for a long time, and he was grateful for him. Even if he was a first-rate dickhead.

"But what does any of this have to do with Maddie?"

"You like her. A lot."

"Sure do."

He liked everything about her. From her soft, straight hair to the sky blue of her eyes, to her pink rosebud of a mouth. He liked the way she laughed and the way she was shy but brave. How she was quietly funny and even how she always seemed a little sad. Liked too how she was kind of absentminded and dreamy. He wanted her to not be afraid to get a little lost because he would always come find her.

"I know. Because I've never seen you like a woman like that."

"The hell is that supposed to mean?" He bristled as he reeled in his line and cast again. "I like a lot of women."

"Oh, I know that too. You love women. But I don't think you've ever loved *a* woman. But I think you might love this one."

Fitz's statement hit him like a flailing fishtail to the face. Did he love Maddie? He sure liked her a lot, wanted to be with her all the time. Wanted her in his bed and over his knee, wanted to guide her and spoil her. Hadn't paid much mind to any of the other myriad women at the Ranch since he set eyes on her.

But that could just mean he had a crush. He'd had those, lots of times. And look where that had led him. Standing in the middle of a river, fly-fishing with his buddy because he'd fucked his way through a good portion of this big-sky, big-ass state.

"What if I just like her? What if she's the same as all the rest?"

Reid shook his head as soon as he said it because that wasn't fair. If there was one thing he knew, it was that the problem had never been the women he was with but him. He was the one with the short attention span, he was the one who could turn on a dime, he was the one who was all wham-bam-thank-you-ma'am and on to the next.

"That's what I'm trying to tell you, but you're not picking up what I'm putting down. I know you think of yourself as some fickle drifter. Your dad sure made you feel like a derelict for leaving home. And you know, you might fuck around with your job, your friends, your hobbies, women, where you live. But once you find what you're looking for, I don't think there's anything that could pry you loose. It's like you've got to throw a lot of spaghetti at the wall, but when something sticks, it's stuck. Like your job. Like being my friend. And I'd be willing to bet a whole lot that if you let yourself really be Maddie Arsenault's Daddy? You're never gonna want anything or anyone else."

The water rushed around the thighs of his waders, and the sun beat down hot, warming his face and arms. The air was cool from the movement of the river, and the spray from the rapids cooled his skin as he listened to the various critters chirping and peeping and making their other little critter noises. It all felt real right, one of the things he loved about being out on rivers. All different but all the same, they all lent him the kind of peace he'd been looking for all his life. He didn't feel restless or unhappy when he was casting his line. And while he'd prefer to have a dinner of fresh fish to show for it, he wouldn't call a day out on the river wasted even if he came home with an empty basket.

It should've scared him half to death, the idea that Maddie might be the one. It sounded absurd that he could meet a woman one day and less than a week later know he wanted her to belong to him forever. But maybe it wasn't so ridiculous; maybe that's just how he was wired. Being with Maddie felt as right as being out on the river.

* * *

"I THINK I might be falling for Reid."

When Tamsyn gave her a "please, girl" look, Maddie had to concede. "Fine. I have fallen for him. Is that what you wanted to hear?"

"Well, it's nice. Seeing you happy for the first time in five years."

"It's nice to be happy," Maddie murmured, playing over the past week in her mind. Except for falling off Star. That hadn't been any fun at all. But the part where Reid had fussed over her and cared for her afterward had made her feel pretty good.

"Seriously, what's not to like? He's hot, he's super into you, he wants to spend all his time with you but also understands home fries come before guys, and he's a total Daddy."

It was true. Reid was basically perfect but not in a way that felt too good to be true. Except for one thing.

"But he lives in Montana. And I live in Penshaw. If I thought either of those things would change, then maybe we could do the long-distance thing for a while until we could be together, but..."

She shrugged and felt unexpectedly hollow inside. She was pretty used to her heart feeling like a desolate landscape with only the occasional tumbleweed rolling through, but this was different. Deeper, sharper, a pang that cut into a tender part of her that had been dormant.

The idea of not being with Reid anymore *hurt*.

"First off, I think that man would move to the moon for you if you asked him to."

A warm glow trickled up from her chest to her cheeks because she was pretty sure Tamsyn was right. Reid would do anything for her, even leave his beloved big-sky country. If she asked him to. Could she ask him to?

They'd only known each other a week, and forever hadn't been the plan at all. But what was the worst thing that could happen if she asked? He'd say no? She wouldn't be any worse off than she was now. She could also tell herself his rejection wasn't about her, because what kind of sensible person uprooted their life and moved halfway across the country for a girl they'd just met? She liked that Reid was practical and down-to-earth. It was a nice balance to her inclination to always have her head in the clouds. She wouldn't ask him to betray his nature.

Her internal hemming and hawing got interrupted by her bestie's musings.

"But also, you could move out here. I mean, honestly, now that I'm headed to the East Coast, there's nothing to keep you in Penshaw."

Tamsyn's words landed like a punch to the gut. Oof.

"Nothing?" Maddie echoed, staring into space, seeing all her happy memories with Josh flashing before her eyes. They were all in Penshaw. Holding hands in the bleachers at homecoming, taking a walk together along the river that ran through the center of town, the night she lost her virginity on a blanket under the stars out by the reservoir, kissing him goodbye at the curb before he got on the bus to leave for basic training, never to return again. Josh's grave that she visited on his birthday and holidays and anytime she was feeling really lonely, which was often. Everything, *everything* was there.

"My whole life is there. You're leaving, and that's shitty as hell, but at least I can go visit you or you can come see me after you go. But otherwise, everything that's important to me is still there. How can you say that's nothing?"

It wasn't fair to be getting shrill and angry with her best friend, but her feelings all felt so close to the surface these days. Some of them closer than others.

In that moment she realized happiness and contentment had been overtaking grief and heartache since she'd been with Reid, and it turned her world upside down.

"Maddie, I didn't mean it like that, and you know it. Come on, don't be upset. I'm just happy for you, that's all."

"Yeah, I know, but it…"

It didn't feel right. It didn't feel right to be happy, to be shedding the cloak of her grief. To even consider the possibility of leaving Penshaw, of leaving the only shreds of Josh she had left. She was a terrible, faithless person. Josh deserved better. Reid deserved better.

Was it fair to demand Reid uproot his very real and actually existent life because of her attachment to and preoccupation with Josh? A dead man? A ghost? She might not like the answer, but she knew what it was.

"I'm going to go for a walk. Maybe I'll see you at the barbecue."

And without giving Tamsyn a chance to distract her, Maddie walked out.

CHAPTER 24

Reid was ambling with Fitz toward where the big barbecue had been set up when he saw Maddie leaving the main resort building, headed in the opposite direction. She was too far for him to read the expression on her face, but there was something about the way she moved that said everything was not right with the world.

He and Fitz exchanged looks, and his friend shrugged. "You better go get your girl."

That was one of the things he appreciated about Fitz. He might be a meddling punk ass, but he believed in their friendship, in Reid's trueheartedness. He never acted like any shiny thing he chased after was a threat to their bond. Was also of the firm opinion that Maddie wasn't just another sparkly distraction.

"Catch you later," Reid told him with a punch to his biceps and jogged after his little wanderer.

Didn't take him long to catch up with her, but she didn't turn around when he did, even though she must've heard him.

"Maddie-girl, where you off to? You know you're not supposed to wander alone."

She turned to him, hands clenched in front of her embroidered denim skirt. "Just, um, away."

"That doesn't sound fun. Definitely doesn't sound as tasty as the barbecue. Come on, let's walk over together."

Reid offered her his arm, like a damn gentleman, but instead of smiling and hooking her hand through the crook of his elbow, Maddie shook her head.

"Thanks for the offer, but I don't want to be around... anyone right now."

He noticed then that there were some dark circles underneath her baby blues and that her face was drawn. She hadn't called him *Daddy* either.

"You alright? Your arm hurting too much for you to sleep? You seemed fine last night."

And the night before. And the night before that. Those precious nights when she'd fallen asleep in his arms.

"Oh no," she said, shaking her head again. "I mean, it still hurts a little, but it doesn't keep me up at night. Promise."

"Then what's goin' on, darlin'? Don't you tell me *nothing*. I can see better than that, and you know what happens to Little girls who tell lies. And who wander off."

Her cheeks flushed the same shade of pink as he'd turned her backside the other day.

"Please don't, Reid. I'm not in the mood for... I can't..."

That's when the first tear spilled out the corner of her eye, and his heart sank. He hadn't meant to make her cry, and now he definitely wasn't going to let her go without an explanation.

"I'm not in the habit of letting pretty girls go wandering

off to cry. You're gonna come sit and tell me what these waterworks are all about. No arguments."

He scooped up her hand and led her over to a swing hanging from a sturdy tree branch, picked her up by her hips, then plopped her onto the wide wood plank and stood between her knees. She winced from the impact but didn't hiss; her bruises must be fading.

Maddie wrapped her hands around the ropes that held the swing aloft, and he could see the little suns and rainbows someone had painted on her fingernails. This girl was so precious it was going to do him in.

She didn't look at him but stared off into the dirt to his right. Even without being able to look into her eyes, he could tell she was real sad about something. Her tears and her downcast expression didn't seem angry or frustrated in that spiky, tense way. Just a whole lot of hollow-stomached, soul-smushed sad.

"What's going on, darlin'?"

When she still didn't meet his eyes, he took her trembling chin between his thumb and his knuckle then tipped her face up toward where the sun was setting. The pink glow made the tear tracks on her cheeks look glossy, and he wanted to kiss them away.

"Come on, talk to Daddy."

That's when the floodgates opened.

* * *

HE HELD HER, rubbed her back while she sobbed, but she didn't let herself cry it all the way out, he could tell. She was stiff and real sniffly when she pulled away, took the handkerchief from his hand instead of allowing him to wipe her face.

Reid hated it, but he would keep that to his damn self for now. He could sense she wasn't going to talk to him if he pushed, so he waited. Patience wasn't always his strong suit, but for Maddie? He'd wait until the end of his days.

It paid off when she finally started to talk, even if she was looking down at the dirt instead of at him.

"I was dating this boy in high school. My parents didn't like him, but all they could see was that he was rough around the edges. Wasn't from the right part of town. Josh didn't think he was smart because he didn't do well in school, but that was just because he didn't learn very well from books and lectures. He was…he was more like you."

Maddie blinked up at him, and he could see there was so much pain in her eyes, so much hurt.

"Grease monkey?" he offered with a little smile and a rub of his thumb over her knuckles. Even with a whole bunch of scrubbing, his nails weren't completely clean, and he felt extra big and extra dirty in front of this pretty and petite woman.

She repaid him with a sheepish smile of her own, and he grinned back to let her know he wasn't offended. He knew what he was, and he was fine with it. Meant he wouldn't mind scrapping and sweating, whatever he needed to do to keep this Little girl safe and happy.

"Yeah. Like he could take stuff apart and put it back together, he could fix almost anything, he could build things without instructions. And no, he didn't have the best manners, but he was so sweet to me."

Huh. Josh the grease monkey, his Little girl's first love. Maddie was definitely the sensitive type, but unless something real bad had happened, he couldn't imagine her still pining for her high school sweetheart.

"He joined the army the day after we graduated. I didn't

go to college since he promised, once he had some money saved up, we'd get married and I could go live with him. I liked the idea of moving around because I'd grown up in Penshaw and kind of expected to die there without having done much of anything in between. And I liked the idea of being one of those army wives with a jumble of kids, a houseful of children to keep me busy, keep me company. My house had always been so lonely, and I wanted some noise. Plus, he told me the military's like a big family. You move somewhere new, there are always people who will help you out even if they don't know you from Adam. Sounded pretty good to me."

It was hard to listen to her talk about a man she'd clearly loved with all her heart. Hard to watch her conjure up a future that had nothing to do with him, Reid. But he was fairly certain where this story was headed, and his heart ached for her already.

"So I waited. Through basic training, through him getting his first post. He was so excited because he got assigned to be a wheeled vehicle mechanic and loved it. His chain of command was really impressed with him too. After a lifetime of people acting like he wasn't much of anything, he felt like he was doing something important. Like he was making a difference."

Reid could understand that. Hell, he'd felt that way himself after he left his family's ranch. He couldn't wait to prove that he could be good at something and stick with it. Earn his parents' acceptance and pride. Maybe make a woman like Maddie look at him like he was a big man someday. Yep, that all felt real familiar.

"He got killed in action recovering a vehicle that had seen combat. It was hard to watch my parents be relieved since they hadn't wanted me to marry him. And to have people tell me I was so young and I'd find someone new. I didn't want to find someone new. Of course, Tamsyn was better than that because she's awesome."

"She's a real good friend to you," he murmured, understanding maybe for the first time how deep the bond between the two women went.

"She's the best," Maddie agreed with a decisive nod. "But even with her... I never told her Josh was my Daddy. She obviously figured it out eventually, but she didn't know back then. It was something Josh and I were still figuring out and muddling through, and I was so self-conscious about it. It still felt kinda wrong, you know? So I didn't tell her because even though I thought she'd understand, I wasn't a hundred percent sure. I couldn't stand the idea of losing my best friend on top of losing Josh. So I kept my mouth shut. And since we weren't married and I didn't live on base, I didn't have that army family to support me either."

Poor Little girl, mourning her Daddy all alone. The thought of Maddie curled around Cleopatra and sobbing because her Daddy was gone and never coming back broke his heart.

She was too pure for this world to start, and the one person who'd understood she needed someone to protect and discipline her, to be both gentle and rough, to keep all the bad things away had been taken away himself. Left her all alone in this big bad world, and she'd just been trying to make it through ever since, no Daddy at her side to help guide her through. That would explain the air of sadness she always seemed to have about her. She missed her Daddy.

So where did that leave them? His first instinct as a mechanic was always to root out the problem and fix it, get the motor purring again. But how did a man fix a Little girl's broken heart? Especially if she didn't want it to be fixed.

He'd thought they'd had a real good week together. If he was being completely honest, it'd been incredible. Perfect. He hadn't thought he'd been alone in feeling that way.

While it had taken Maddie a bit to warm up to him, their time together—when it wasn't scorching hot—had felt like he was basking in the glow of a crackling fire after coming in from the cold. Did she feel differently? Could he even ask her? It felt rude somehow, like he'd be trying to elbow the memory of Josh aside and shout in her face, *What about me?*

He didn't want to do that to either of them. He also didn't want to walk away from a Little girl who would maybe appreciate a hand out of the pit of despair she seemed lost in. Worst pickle he'd ever found himself in, with the highest stakes too. One step wrong and he could lose the best thing that'd ever happened to him.

CHAPTER 25

It was hard talking about Josh. It was always hard, and she'd mostly stopped doing it. Partly because almost no one wanted to hear it five years on if they'd ever wanted to in the first place, but also because it never seemed to make anything better. Heck, maybe it was a mistake to tell Reid. But he'd asked and she couldn't refuse him.

His eyes might be a shade of ice, but they felt warm with compassion as he gazed at her. Maybe some pity too, but she'd take that. She was pitiful and she knew it.

She also liked Reid—a lot. More than she'd liked anyone since Josh. It wouldn't do to have Reid thinking he wasn't good enough for her. Because she was fairly certain they'd passed the charade that this was just a week of fun some time ago. Maybe around when he'd said he loved her. Well, *Daddy* loved her, which was different, but she suspected only a little.

"I've never gotten over it. Or moved on."

She shrugged, and Reid's brows formed an indignant V.

"I hate how people say that. Like grief is an object instead of something that stays with you. Might feel smaller, or maybe your world gets bigger, but I don't think that kind of loss ever really leaves a body."

Reid had proved himself sensitive and caring over their time together, but she still didn't expect something so deeply compassionate to come out of his mouth. Then again, people tended to underestimate the emotional capacity of grease monkeys. She would know.

"Yeah. It's still right here," she said, putting a hand over her heart where she swore the organ ached. "And it still hurts. So much. I've really enjoyed spending the week with you. More than I've enjoyed anything in a long time. But I'm not sure where this—you and me—could possibly go."

It felt terrible to say that out loud, to Reid's face. Awful to see the flash of hurt in his eyes.

She didn't think he'd lash out and yell at her or anything like that, but she still wanted to run away. What was the point of talking about this anymore? She wasn't going to change, and he couldn't possibly accept coming in second place to a corpse five years in the grave. That should pretty well spell the end.

"How come?" he asked, his voice soft. "Does your past with Josh keep you from seeing a future with me?"

"Yes?"

Maddie didn't mean for it to come out as a question. God knew she'd never questioned her fate before.

"Can you tell me why?" he prodded. "I'm not trying to change your mind. I'm just trying to understand. Because the truth is that even though we haven't spent all that long together, you've become real special to me. I didn't know if I'd ever find a woman who would hold my attention, but I've got to say you've done more than that. You've captured my heart."

Reid pressed his palm against hers and then laced their

fingers together. This damn cowboy, always making her weepy.

"That's why it's so awful," she wailed. "Because I feel the same way."

Her chin trembled uncontrollably, and she started crying again.

"That does sound awful," he teased gently.

"You're not awful. You're wonderful. You've been the best Daddy this whole week, and I think about what it would be like for you to be my Daddy for longer than that all the time."

"How much longer?"

"A lot longer."

"Maybe forever longer?" Reid offered, and she shook her head. That was too far. Too much to ask. Too much to give.

"Reid, please don't."

"Why not, little girl? All I want to do is make you happy."

She'd heard people describe having hope as their hearts soaring. She wished Reid's words gave her heart wings, and maybe they did, but she was still burdened by so much sadness. So much grief. She just couldn't wish for happiness or even hope. That would mean abandoning the man who'd loved her most.

* * *

MADDIE SHOOK HER HEAD, so much sadness in her face he didn't know how she could hold it all. When she met his gaze, she whispered, "I feel so guilty, like I'm betraying him."

No wonder she couldn't think about a future with him,

Reid. Not if she thought it meant she had to throw away her past, act as though she'd shaken off the grief of losing the man who'd been her Daddy. It wouldn't be fair to ask her for that, and he wouldn't. She should know that.

"Oh, darlin'. You don't have any less love in your heart for Josh than you ever did. That's not how love works. There's just more of it. I would never ask you to forget about him. Hell, I love that man myself for taking such good care of you. But you can't tell me he's wishing from heaven that you'll be alone for the rest of your life. Josh sounds like a real good man who wanted you to be happy and safe and loved more than anything else in this world. I think he's still wishing that."

"You do?" She sniffed.

"'Course I do."

Uncertainty made her eyes wide and pleading. She needed more than that from him, and he wouldn't withhold it.

"Was Josh selfish?"

"No," she insisted, shaking her head and making those pigtails swing around her shoulders. "He loved his family. He loved his country. He loved me."

"Did he want what was best for you?"

"Always. He said if I wanted to go to college before we got married that he'd wait for me. He said if I really didn't want him to join up because I'd worry too much, he wouldn't. Even though he wanted to serve more than almost anything else."

"Was he jealous?"

That made her pause for a second, but he waited, suspecting what the answer would be.

"I wouldn't say *jealous*. He didn't worry when I talked to other boys because he knew I was his. And he didn't get mad when I spent time with my friends or my family. I might call him possessive, though. Not in a bad way. He just liked people knowing I was his."

"You think he's jealous of me?"

Maddie rolled her lips between her teeth, and her chin wrinkled as her eyes watered. "No. Maybe envious because you can touch me and he can't. Because you have time with me he never got."

"I can live with envy," he told her gently as he thumbed away tears that had started rolling down her cheeks. "And I can live with you missing him. What I don't think I can live without is you."

She blinked at him with those big blue eyes, and suddenly he wanted to share with her as much as she'd shared with him.

"There's no reason why you'd know this, but I've got sort of a reputation back home as a ladies' man. I've dated a lot of women, slept with a lot more. I'm not saying that to make you jealous or feel like you're lucky. It's just facts."

He pulled their joined hands to his mouth, kissed along Maddie's knuckles.

"And I've been kind of a drifter. Lived in a lot of different towns, had a bunch of different jobs. But I love being a mechanic, can't imagine doing anything else with my life. Not every day is easy, but I always feel like I accomplished something, and there's a lot of contentment to be had from fixing broken things. Or keeping things in good condition so they don't break in the first place."

His Little girl's head was tilted to the side as she listened, and she was just too sweet for words. Even with her face blotchy from all her tears, he'd never seen anyone prettier.

"I like Almandine, and I'll probably always want to live

somewhere kind of wild with big skies, but my heart's not set on that town. Or this state, even though I've lived here my whole life. Someday I'll find the place where I'm meant to be. Somewhere that makes me feel as at home and satisfied as I do working at Mason's. As much as I do when I'm with you."

Reid was good at flirting, skilled in the art of seduction, but clearly he needed some work on telling the woman he loved the way he felt. On the other hand, he'd never had to do it before, and he hoped to never have to do it quite this way ever again. He ran a frustrated hand through his hair and then took both of Maddie's hands in his, looking her right in her wide-open eyes.

"What I'm trying to say is that I'm a rolling stone and you make me want to grow moss. I don't slow down for hardly anything, but once something is right, it's right. You're right for me, Maddie-girl. I can feel it in my bones, and they've never lied to me."

* * *

MADDIE HAD NEVER THOUGHT of moss as romantic. But then again, she'd never met Reid Phillips before this week.

In her heart, she could feel that what he said was true, and she felt the same. Maybe that's what her heart had been trying to tell her this whole time. Maybe she'd never felt this way about anyone since Josh because she hadn't met anyone who could be right for her since Josh.

She believed Reid when he promised he didn't want her to forget about Josh. He seemed to understand how much Josh had meant to her. Meant to her still. Why she could never be with someone who dismissed her grief or made her feel wrong or crazy for still mourning her loss.

"My heart agrees with your bones," she told him shyly, her stomach all twisted in knots.

"I'm awful glad to hear that. And maybe you'll think I'm crazy—hell, maybe I am—but once I find what's right, I don't want to go any longer than I have to without it in my life. I love living out here, but I'd move to Ohio for you, little girl. Can't imagine Mason's would be real happy to lose me and without a lot of notice, but I could probably find a job around Penshaw pretty easy. Good mechanics are hard to find."

"You would do that? But you love Montana. You just said so yourself."

"I do," he conceded. "But I love you more."

Wow.

"And besides, it's not real proper for a Daddy to live fifteen hundred miles away from his Little girl. Wouldn't seem right to me either for a man to live half a country away from his wife."

His what now?

"Are you—are you asking me to marry you?"

Reid pressed kisses to the backs of her hands before he got down on one knee in front of her, the denim of his jeans pressing into the dirt. Well, he'd probably gotten out worse stains from the shop, and maybe she should forget about laundry for a second and pay attention to the man who seemed to be proposing to her. Talk about priorities.

"I am now."

He took a deep breath, probably trying to gather his thoughts, and Maddie tried to remember to breathe. It wasn't easy.

"Maddie, you're the prettiest girl I've ever seen. You're sweet and funny and a bit of a dreamer. I love that you always try your best to be a good girl, and your submission makes me feel like I'm ten feet tall. It's harder for me to imagine living without you than it is for me to imagine not living in Montana. I want to spend the rest of my life taking care of you and loving on you, disciplining you and supporting you. I swear I will try to be the Daddy you deserve for the rest of my days. Madigan Rose Arsenault, will you marry me?"

It felt like her heart was getting reamed out by a citrus juicer. How could something so wonderful hurt so badly? But she knew why, and now so did Reid. Which was probably why he pressed another kiss to the back of her hand.

When he did, a whole lot of memories fell on her like rain. Her and Josh. Her and Reid. Tender times, steamy times, the good and the bad, the joyous and the grave. She could see how alike Josh and Reid were in some ways but also how they were so different. She could also picture Josh looking down on them now, shaking his head and saying, "Don't you dare let me be the reason you keep yourself from bliss, Maddie Rose."

Reid was right. It would be so like Josh to insist on her happiness, to put her peace and safety before all other things. Josh would've liked Reid if they'd had a chance to meet. She'd like to think he would trust the man in front of her to provide everything he couldn't anymore. She wanted to believe that even if there was envy, there could be compersion as well.

"Take your time, darlin'. I know you weren't expecting this today and maybe never. And I understand if you need a bit to figure out if this can work. There's lots to be sorted out. I don't expect you to be as impulsive as me, so—"

"Yes," she blurted out.

Their faces must've been mirror images of shock because she'd sure surprised herself too.

"Yes?" Reid echoed cautiously. "Are you sure? I—"

"Yes, I'm sure. Yes, I want to marry you."

She climbed off the swing and perched on her Daddy's thigh so she could hug him, wrapping her arms around his neck and feeling his heartbeat, steady and strong and true. Feeling his arms, solid and warm, around her waist.

Loving him didn't mean loving Josh any less. While it was hard to believe she'd gotten so lucky in her one precious life as to have not one soul mate but two, she wasn't going to let Reid ride off into the sunset without her at his side.

"I love you, Daddy."

"I love you too, my forever little girl."

EPILOGUE

Last night after Maddie had agreed to be his bride, they'd walked around the Ranch for hours. Talking about the past, making plans for the future. They'd ended up down by the lake, watching fireflies flicker in the brush.

It had been quiet and peaceful and private, and now that was over. So very over.

Maddie had told Tamsyn about their engagement and he'd told Fitz, and then their two bigmouthed best friends had told many, many people. So many people in fact that Derek had insisted on having a champagne toast at the farewell brunch on Tuesday morning.

Well, champagne or mimosas for the Bigs and the Littles who had permission. Sparkling apple cider or plain OJ for the other Littles.

"Just the one glass," he'd murmured to Maddie when they'd clinked the narrow flutes of champagne the waitstaff had handed out. "And sip it real slow. There won't be any drunken shenanigans on my watch, understand?"

"Yes, Daddy," his little darlin' had agreed with a pretty blush on the apples of her cheeks.

They'd actually found a moment to eat some of their meal between well-wishers crowding their table, so they were attempting to shovel various brunch foods into their mouths when Sadie Hawkins plopped into the empty seat next to Tamsyn.

"Ah, this is awesome! Daddy makes the best matches. You two are going to be happy forever!"

Reid smiled around his mouthful of maple-pork sausage and hoped he wasn't being too rude. But damn was he hungry. After all that walking last night, he'd taken Maddie back to his room and had his way with her. A few times. And again before breakfast.

He should be more mindful of letting his Little girl get her rest, but he hadn't been able to help himself. He was just in such damn high spirits that everyone here should be thankful he was refraining from bending Maddie over their dining table.

Sadie leaned over Tamsyn to whisper to Maddie, and he could only make out a few words, including: "It's really more of a tradition." Whatever the hell that meant.

Then Derek was settling into the chair next to his Little wife and using a firm grip on her bouncy ponytail to pull her away from Maddie.

"Sadie Marie, I know you're not trying to involve Maddie in any more of your shenanigans."

Sadie opened her mouth to argue, but Derek raised his stern brows. "Saying 'it's more of a tradition' will not save your backside from a well-deserved spanking, little girl."

Maddie giggled as Sadie snapped her mouth shut and pursed her lips in a pout.

His mischievous Little tamed for the moment, Derek turned his attention to Reid and Maddie, giving them a wide, sincere smile.

"Congratulations, you two. I couldn't be happier this worked out the way it did. Beautiful couple—you're going to be very happy together."

"Thank you, Derek. And thank you for trusting me to be this Little girl's Daddy this week. I don't think we ever would've found our way to each other otherwise."

The big man smiled like the cat who'd caught the canary. "Matchmaking is a hobby of mine. Always a joy to see another happy couple start their journey here."

Sadie had apparently tired of being quiet and started rapid-firing questions at them.

"When are you getting married? Where are you getting married? Oh, are you gonna do it here? You should have it here. Weddings are the best. Can I be a bridesmaid? Did he give you a ring? Is he going to? Where are you going to live? How is that going to work? Are you gonna wait to have babies or—"

"Hush, little girl, before I take you over my knee for being nosy. I'm sure Reid and Maddie have a lot to talk about, and we're not going to get all up in their business," Derek told his wife, and then with a glance to Reid and Maddie, he added, "Unless, of course, they want to share."

Reid held Maddie's hand under the table and gave her a squeeze.

"Well, since Maddie was going to have to find a smaller place with Tamsyn leaving for Clover City, she decided, instead of moving to another apartment in Penshaw, that she was gonna come out here, see how she feels about being a Montanan. Aren't you, darlin'?"

"Yes, Daddy."

She squeezed his hand back, and he knew even though she was excited about living with him, it was going to be real hard for her to leave Penshaw. He'd already promised they could go back to her hometown at least once a year on a date of her choosing, and that had eased her anxiety a bit. And who knew? If she moved out here and hated it, he sure wasn't in the business of making his Little girl miserable. They'd move back to Ohio and come visit Montana instead. What mattered most was that they'd be together.

"We haven't set a date yet," Maddie said, "but we'll probably get married in Penshaw. My folks don't get around very well anymore, and I know they'd hate to miss their only child's wedding."

Reid knew it had to do with feeling like she had Josh's blessing too, but they didn't need to share that with the whole world.

"I guess that makes sense," grumbled Sadie, who then perked up when Maddie went on.

"But we talked about coming back here for our honeymoon."

"Oooh, yes! Honeymoons are even better than weddings. You're going to have so much fun here."

"That's the idea, yes," he drawled, leaning over to kiss his fiancée's cheek. Fiancée. He liked the sound of that. Not as well as *wife*, but it would do until he could get his Little darlin' down the aisle.

"I hope the wedding party's invited," Tamsyn told Maddie with a smirk, making his Little girl blush to within an inch of her life. "Not to, like, the actual sex stuff—"

Beside him Fitz raised a hand. "I would like to be invited to the actual sex stuff."

That earned him a swift elbow to the ribs from Reid while Sadie giggled and even Derek chuckled.

"You can come to the Ranch for the honeymoon," Reid told his best man, "but you're gonna have to figure out your own sex stuff."

"I'll take it."

God help him with these people, but he wouldn't trade them for anything. He tapped his glass softly with his knife, and when the people at their table had settled down, he raised his glass.

"I wanted to make a toast to my lovely bride-to-be, the best friends anyone could ask for, and the most magical place on earth. I'm the luckiest man alive, and this has turned out to be one memorable Memorial Day."

THE END

To read more from Rawhide Ranch, go to https://readerlinks.com/l/2415889.

I HOPE you loved watching Reid and Maddie fall in love. Want to know if Tamsyn Yates, Maddie's bestie, gets her own HEA? Just crack that whip, because Tamsyn's book, *Tamsyn's Twin Daddies*, is next in the Clover City Littles series!

Join my newsletter The Hive for all the Must-Know updates. You'll receive a free bonus scene, "Another Memorable Little Memorial Day," when you subscribe: https://readerlinks.com/l/2414725

* * *

IF YOU JUMPED in with Reid and Maddie (and hey, good choice! Who doesn't love Rawhide Ranch?), you've got the whole Clover City Littles series to glom! You can start from the beginning with *Twyla's Teacher Daddy*.

GUNNAR DOESN'T LIKE *brats but maybe Twyla's never had anyone teach her how to be good. Maybe he could be that man. Maybe he could be her daddy.*

* * *

OR MAYBE GLITZ and glam is more your style. You can head straight for the first book in the Bright Lights Little Darlings series, *Ashby's Action Hero Daddy*.

BEING *a superhero on screen doesn't make you man enough to be a little girl's daddy.*

* * *

IF YOU LIKE your heroes rugged and out of uniform, the Frontier Daddies series might be just what you're looking for.

"Daddy's Little Nightingale" is a prequel to the series and is currently published in the Hero Daddies charity anthology for Ukraine. "Daddy's Little One Night Stand" which is currently published in the Nightingale charity anthology for Ukraine, is a prequel to *Daddy's Little Second Chance*, book one in the series.

A NOTE FROM HONEY

Thank you so much for reading *A Memorable Little Memorial Day*! I hope you loved reading Reid and Maddie's story as much as I loved writing it.

If you enjoyed *A Memorable Little Memorial Day*, I would love it if you let your friends know so they can experience Reid and Maddie's relationship too! As with all my books, I've enabled lending to make it easy to share with a friend. If you leave a review for *A Memorable Little Memorial Day* on Amazon, Goodreads, or your own platform, I would love to read it! Send me the link at honeymeyerromance@gmail.com.

You can find the most up to date list of my books on my website: honeymeyerromance.com.

ABOUT HONEY MEYER

Honey Meyer lives in New England, and loves to watch the seasons change outside her window as she writes Happily Ever Afters for littles and their mommies and daddies. She loves to read and write age play romances, and she can't wait to bring you more stories—always sweet with a little sting!

- facebook.com/honeymeyerromance
- twitter.com/SweetHoneyMeyer
- instagram.com/honeymeyerromance
- amazon.com/author/honeymeyer
- bookbub.com/profile/honey-meyer
- goodreads.com/honeymeyerromance

Made in the USA
Coppell, TX
22 July 2024